HELLO, DARKNESS

ANNA MCCLUSKEY

Book 3 of the Mathilda Holiday Series

©2021 Anna McCluskey
Albany, OR

ISBN: 9781734948554
Library of Congress Control Number: 2021919286

All rights reserved. This book or parts thereof may not be reproduced in any form, stored in any retrieval system, or transmitted in any form by any means – electronic, mechanical, photocopy, recording, or otherwise – without prior written permission of the author, except as provided by United States of America copyright law. For permission requests, write to the author at theannafiles@yahoo.com

This is a work of fiction. Any resemblance to actual events, places, or persons, living or dead, is entirely coincidental.

Author website: **www.theannafiles.com**
BookBub: **www.bookbub.com/profile/anna-mccluskey**
Facebook: **www.facebook.com/annamccluskeyauthor**

Cover art by Sleepy Fox Studios
www.sleepyfoxstudios.net

1.

Mattie prowled the area around the old Auditor HQ, trying very hard not to look like she was prowling. She sat on a bench under a streetlight – the sun wasn't quite high enough yet for the lights to turn off – and opened up the newspaper she had been carrying under her arm, feeling completely ridiculous and conspicuous.

She hated guard duty, but everyone had agreed that it was necessary to intercept any Auditor agents who were trying to report in. "Why does that mean I have to dress like an Auditor, though?" she muttered. "And act like I'm in a bad spy movie?"

Did anyone around her actually believe that someone would really be sitting on a bench, reading an actual freaking newspaper, in a crappy neighborhood, at four in the morning, in the twenty-first century, dressed in leather armor? But that's what Sister Margaret had told her to do. And Sister Margaret carried a lot of weapons and seemed like the kind of person who would know how to do reconnaissance.

And the fact remained that, despite the constant presence of police, firefighters, and reporters in the area, no one seemed at all suspicious of her. No one had so much as looked at her askance since she'd started doing this a few days ago, even in broad daylight.

Plus, they had caught four agents who were loyal to the Pontiff and brought in three other agents who were loyal to their rebellion but hadn't been able to get transferred for the battle. So she couldn't argue with efficacy.

And Mattie needed this to work. Even as she disliked what she was doing, she knew she had to do it, that she would do whatever it took to bring down the Auditors – these bastards who hurt her friends, and who had tried to hurt her sister.

She wriggled a little bit on the bench, trying to get the weird leather straps that wrapped across her chest to sit flat. Why would anyone choose to wear this? Mattie longed for a pair of jeans and a cotton t-shirt, preferably one with a band logo or some kind of nerdy quip.

A clanging sound, like a can being kicked, intruded upon her reverie and she turned her head sharply, suddenly laser-focused.

As she scanned the area, Mattie caught a glimpse of a furtive figure skulking in the shadow of a nearby brewery's front patio. The brewpub was closed at this early hour, although she had seen a couple of staff members arrive about thirty minutes ago.

That meant the building was occupied, so she'd have to be careful about window angles as she intercepted the guy.

Mattie turned the page of her newspaper as she surreptitiously studied the crouching man, who was dressed in garb similar to her own and wouldn't look out of place at a renaissance fair.

He looked extremely out of place where he was, however, and was making no effort to fit in as he continued to hide behind a table, staring in shock at the burnt building he'd clearly been heading toward.

The man didn't seem to have noticed her sitting there. Usually, if they saw her outfit, they would assume she was with the organization and approach her.

The Auditor field agents always moved in pairs, which meant that either there was another one around here somewhere, or his partner had been killed in action. Or he wasn't a field agent, but so far no admin agents had shown up with transfer papers – just kidnappers fresh from a job.

Mattie waited a few more moments to see if another agent would show.

The guy didn't seem to be expecting anyone else to turn up, and no one did, so she moved forward with her capture.

Since he wasn't moving anyway, Mattie formed the words of a spell in her mind. Her hands glowed as he froze in place. She folded her newspaper, fighting with the rustling pages in the wind.

Finally, it acquiesced, flattening out, and she carefully hid one hand in its creases and shoved the other into her pocket so no passersby would see them.

Her hands would continue to glow until she released the spell.

She waited a moment to see if anything happened.

If he was a speller, he would still be able to use magic, since spelling was mostly mental and didn't require movement. If he was a stitcher, he wouldn't, since his hands were paralyzed. And if he was a seer, he wouldn't be here, because he would have looked ahead into the future and avoided the place altogether.

After a moment, Mattie rose from her bench and strolled casually toward the patio, deliberately stumbling slightly when she reached the man. She knelt and pretended to tie her shoe as she spoke. "I'm going to release your head from my spell. You won't be able to move your hands, so don't bother trying to stitch. If you try to scream, I'll spell you back to frozen before you get enough out for anyone to notice. Got it?"

Mattie altered the spell and the man nodded. "Who are you?" he asked. "What happened to the HQ?"

"My name is Mattie." She watched his eyes widen. He'd assumed she was an Auditor, of course, and they all went by Agent Whatever-Their-Last-Name-Was.

"Who are you?" he repeated, his voice warier than it had been.

"Where's your partner?" she countered, wanting to make sure he was alone before she went too much further.

The stricken expression on his face was all the answer she needed.

Mattie was torn. On the one hand, if his partner was gone, that was one less agent for her and her allies to deal with.

But she wasn't yet so hardened that she didn't regret the loss of life. After all, technically all of the agents were also victims of the Auditors as a whole.

She hoped that at least whoever they'd been trying to capture had gotten away after killing this guy's partner. If not, then the poor bastard was on a train right now, terrified and confused, on their way to a randomly picked HQ that wasn't this one, to be brainwashed and trained up as another new agent.

"I'm sorry for your loss," she said softly.

His eyes filled with defiance and he straightened his neck as best he could with the rest of his body still held in stasis. "Who. Are. You," he said.

Mattie nodded. Fair enough. "I'm here to offer you a choice. Do you know anyone named Agent Miller?" She kept her voice neutral as she mentioned the name of the former leader of the splinter group whose rebellion she had aided.

The man's eyes narrowed slightly, his head moving into a wary tilt, but he kept his voice measured. "I know three Agent Millers. Which are you talking about?"

"Sure. It's a common name. But I'm pretty sure by the hostility in your voice that you know exactly which Miller I'm talking about."

He turned his head and spat on the ground beside Mattie. "Yeah, we've all heard of her. Her goons approached me once. I told them where that traitor could stick it. Did she do this?"

Mattie grimaced. She stood up and moved away from the gob of spittle, sitting on a bench on one side of a picnic table. She looked around for observers and, seeing none, carefully altered the spell again in her mind, moving the Auditor's limbs into a sitting position and levitating him onto the other bench.

He glared at her. "Answer the question. Is Miller responsible for this and are you with her or with us?"

"Agent Miller is dead," said Mattie bluntly. "Most of the court is also dead. Including the Pontiff. So you can kiss your precious organization as a whole goodbye. We're just mopping up now."

The Auditor's expression froze for a moment before he took a deep, measured breath and arranged his features into careful neutrality. "You're lying."

"I'm not lying, actually. I was there – epic battle, Pontiff beheaded, building exploded, all that jazz. Agent Miller's group has a new leader. They've renounced all ties to the organization and are actively working to destroy what's left of it. As someone who is still part of the organization, that leaves you with two options. Personally, I would suggest the renounce-it-yourself-and-join-us option."

"What's the other one? Die at your hand?" he sneered.

"No. The other is to be taken captive. We'll do our best to reverse your whole brainwashing situation and if we manage it, we might even let you go someday. Meanwhile, you won't be mistreated at all, but you also won't be free."

"I haven't been free in years," he said. "I gave up my freedom willingly to the organization."

"I mean, I don't know that I'd describe being kidnapped and brainwashed as 'willing.'" Mattie raised an eyebrow. "But you are now free to choose. Continue in captivity or help our cause."

"I'd rather die."

Mattie rolled her eyes. These people were always so dramatic. "Well, that's not one of the options available right now. Maybe someday we'll work it into the curriculum."

She pulled her phone out of her back pocket and texted Sister Margaret, letting her know she had a new prisoner for the convent jail.

"Who are you contacting?" the new prisoner demanded. "Where will I be taken?"

"Yeah, I'm not gonna tell you that," said Mattie. She settled in for an awkward wait. It generally took about ten minutes for the nuns to send someone over with their van, and she had to guard the prisoner the whole time and make sure that no one passing by got suspicious. "What's your name?"

"I'm not gonna tell you that," he mocked.

Mattie shrugged. "Suit yourself." She studied his face. "You look like a Steve. I'll just call you Steve."

"You look like an Abomination," he snapped.

"Oh, I am," Mattie agreed. The organization considered anyone an Abomination – capital A every time – who used more than one discipline of magery. "Big time. I haven't figured out the knack for the whole seer-eyes thing, but I'm a natural speller, and I've been stitching for a couple of weeks now, and it's awesome."

Steve stared at her in outrage. "How dare you?" he hissed.

"You used to do it too, right?" Mattie pointed out. "If you hadn't, you wouldn't have gotten yourself kidnapped—"

"Rightfully brought in for re-education," he corrected.

"Potato, potahto," she said. "The point is that you used to morph and it's pretty hypocritical of you to be all judgy at me about it."

"I saw the error of my ways," he said.

"That's one way to look at it." Mattie smiled sadly. "The other way is that a power-hungry group of assholes decided centuries ago to hoard all the power for themselves. And their descendants, who are still going, brainwashed you into doing their dirty work for them. You got any kids?"

Steve's brow furrowed at the sudden change in topic. "No," he answered automatically. "No kids. Why?"

"Well." Mattie leaned forward, catching his eyes in hers. "Did you know that they taught all the kids of the court how to morph?"

"What do you mean by 'morph?'" His frown deepened.

Mattie propped her chin up on her hand. "Morphing is what the court calls their sanctioned use of multiple disciplines. We rescued all of the kids from the court when we attacked—"

"Rescued? You mean kidnapped," said Steve.

"Funny how you interchange those so easily," said Mattie. "We rescued the kids. And every single one of them over the age of eight was being trained to use all three magical disciplines."

"You're lying again," said Steve.

"Nope, I'm really not," said Mattie. "Still feeling super loyal to those court assholes?"

He didn't answer, turning his head away from her instead, looking toward the burnt building across and down the street.

Mattie picked up her phone again, giving Steve some time with his thoughts, letting doubts sink into his mind. Already, two of the agents they'd taken captive were starting to show signs of switching their allegiance. Maybe Steve could see the light too.

She idly scrolled through her email, pausing at one from her ex-husband. Their divorce court date was coming up soon. Craig's email was titled simply, "Fuck You."

That seemed about right. Mattie decided her day was going to be long and stressful enough without dealing with him.

She kept scrolling. Funny how all of the emails were from her old life – the vice principal of the school she used to teach at in Portland.

The property management company she used to rent from, giving her formal notice that she was officially evicted.

Ah, yes, another one from Craig. Upon reflection, the angry title of his most recent email might have been a reaction to all of these other emails going unanswered.

Whatever. She had more important shit to do.

An unmarked white van pulled up beside them, and Mattie closed out the app and slipped the phone back into her pocket. She stood and grinned at the driver, who gave her a jaunty wave.

The door opened and Sister Margaret hopped out, engine still running.

If anyone had told Mattie a month before that she was shortly going to meet a nun who would quickly become one of her best friends, she would have assumed they were on drugs or had her confused with someone else. But Sister Margaret wasn't your stereotypical nun.

She was dressed a lot like Mattie, but she moved comfortably in her leather, somehow managing to look graceful and athletic as she buckled on a belt with two swords hanging from it while she jumped out of the van, her long black braid swinging over her shoulder.

"Hola, chica! You nabbed another one, huh? Well done!" Sister Margaret lifted her hand, and Mattie high-fived her with a resounding smack. "He got a name?"

"I'm calling him Steve," said Mattie.

Sister Margaret raised a perfectly shaped eyebrow. "A first name? I thought you said he was loyal to the organization."

Mattie shrugged. "He wouldn't tell me his real name."

The nun cackled. "He does look like a Steve." She paused and her eyes went totally white as she turned on her seer sight to look into the future. "There's a cop coming around the corner. How about a sight shield?"

The glow around Mattie's hands pulsed as she added another spell, this one hiding the three of them from any passersby. It was a tricky spell, and she felt the strain as she held it alongside the paralysis spell she already had going.

"Hurry, please," she said, gritting her teeth.

Sister Margaret nodded and leaned across the front seat of the van to pull a handful of zip ties out of the center console.

Mattie glanced around as the police car rounded the corner, just as Sister Margaret had predicted.

The car drove slowly up the street, the officer inside scanning the area in a lackadaisical manner.

Turning her attention back to the task at hand, Mattie watched Sister Margaret quickly and expertly wrap the ties around the captive's left hand, forcing the fingers together so he couldn't make the arcane gestures needed to stitch.

Suddenly, Sister Margaret's head snapped back as Steve punched his hands upward. "What the fuck?" yelled Sister Margaret as she stumbled backward, drawing her twin swords as she quickly regained her balance.

Mattie stared at the prisoner, frozen in place, her eyes wide.

Her spell hadn't been broken – the Auditor shouldn't have been able to move.

"A little help here, Mattie?" called Sister Margaret as she ducked Steve's punches and kicks. She had reverted her eyes to normal sight for some reason, which seemed like an odd choice in the middle of a fight.

"Yes! Sorry!" Mattie charged toward the fight, tackling the Auditor and wrestling him to the ground, for once glad of the leather armor she wore, as her hands scraped against the concrete, but her arms and legs were protected.

Mattie managed to get herself on top of him, pinning him to the ground.

Then she caught sight of his eyes and reeled backward – they were filled with an inky blackness, the opposite of how a seer's eyes looked when they used their mage powers.

While she was distracted, Steve managed to wriggle one arm out from Mattie's grasp and she instinctively bucked her head downward as he rose, smashing her forehead into him. As dumb luck would have it, he had been turning his head slightly, and she hit his temple instead of smacking forehead-to-forehead.

He went limp, his disturbingly black eyes closing.

Mattie sat back, clutching her head with both hands. "Why the fuck did I do that?" she yelled.

Sister Margaret grinned, sheathing her swords. "Oh, you'll be fine. It's one of those things that hurts like a bitch for a few minutes and then starts to ebb. Like stubbing your toe."

Mattie glared at the warrior nun. "What the hell happened back there?"

"Honestly?" Sister Margaret reached down and Mattie grasped her calloused hand gratefully, pulling herself to her feet. "I have no idea. I've never seen anything like that."

"My spell just stopped working!" Speaking of which… Mattie dropped the immobilization spell that she was still holding over Steve. No point in wasting energy.

Sister Margaret nodded. "So did my sight," she said grimly. "It looked like he was just frozen in time. That has never happened before. And it only applied to him. Everything else was moving normally in seer mode." She gestured toward the police car, which had circled back around and was driving by again, its bright light pointed right at them as it passed by. "Your sight shield seems to be holding, so at least something's going right. Did you see his eyes?"

Mattie shuddered. "It was so creepy. What causes that?"

"I don't know," said Sister Margaret. She quickly, almost convulsively, drew her right hand in the sign of the cross, touching her forehead, chest, and each shoulder in succession. "I've been a mage since I was a little girl and a warrior for over a decade. I've never seen anything like this."

Mattie opened her mouth to reply, but before she could, Sister Margaret's eyes widened, fixing on something behind Mattie.

The warrior nun drew her twin swords again, shoving Mattie out of the way with an elbow as she charged forward. "We've got another one!" she called out.

***

Tillie, Mattie's identical twin sister, was also awake, despite the early hour. She wandered around her condo in her skimpy blue silk nightie, loathe to acknowledge that it was now technically morning and that if she was actually "up" she should really change into her workout clothes and get her day started.

She'd been awake for a couple of hours at this point, first waking at the sound of a slamming door in another condo, then tossing and turning for about an hour, before getting up to pee and never going back to bed.

She had just been pacing between the kitchen and her bedroom, lost in thought and constantly glancing into the now-empty guest room that lived between.

Until three days ago, Mattie had been staying in that room. Then she had moved into a small house with two of the rebel Auditor agents, and the condo, which had formerly been Tillie's sanctuary, her haven of solitude, had become somehow both echoingly empty and terrifyingly populated by monsters around every corner at the same time.

She drifted into the living room and touched a discreet button on her entertainment center. The doors of the cabinet slid open with a small whooshing sound, revealing the hidden television set.

Tillie sank down onto the couch, leaning forward to open the drawer of her distressed-wood coffee table and grab the remote. She hit power and the TV turned on to reveal an anchorwoman seated behind a desk. A familiar scene floated in a square image just above the reporter's left shoulder.

Tillie turned up the volume to better hear the news.

" —city police are still looking for any information on the bizarre events of last Friday night, when a midtown building was destroyed by a mysterious fire, killing several hundred people who were gathered in a large banquet hall. Police have identified the building as being owned by a Belgium-based accountancy corporation called Magi Auditing. Police say that the fire was likely started on purpose.

"A spokesperson from the company says that the building was their local corporate headquarters and was used for office space and as temporary living quarters for visiting staff. She has expressed bafflement that anyone would target the building, and has said that their own internal security is also investigating. KFYP's own Stacy Polk is on location. Stacy?"

The screen changed to show the ash-streaked stone façade of the Auditor building. Tillie's breath caught, and she forced herself to breathe evenly. She barely heard the reporter as she began to speak, vaguely hearing her speculating about what kind of gathering had been going on, and the odd way the victims were dressed.

Tillie found herself transfixed instead by the empty gap where the grand wooden double doors had been in the front of the building and the smoke stains on the grey stone around it.

She jumped to her feet again and strode to the antique desk in the corner of the room, sitting down on the padded wooden seat and pulling a notebook toward her. She grabbed a pencil.

If a spokesperson from this Belgian company – which had to be a front for the Auditor organization – was involved, that meant there was still some kind of core leadership left, and it meant that the leadership was aware of what had happened in St. Louis.

The buffer of time they'd thought they had for regrouping and planning their next move had just disappeared.

Tillie began writing down the facts of the situation. As a natural seer, she tended to live more in the future and plan things out. It always helped her to have the past and present details written down so she didn't have to constantly remember them.

The facts were grim. They'd started out with around three hundred rebel Auditors. Forty-six of those had fallen in battle, a number that was etched into the minds of all the survivors. In theory, that left around two hundred and fifty. But a good half of those had elected to return to their former lives as soon as the battle was over.

Tillie couldn't blame them. They had never chosen the life of an agent. If she'd been kidnapped and brainwashed, she'd probably want to go back to normalcy as soon as she could too.

And many of the ones who'd gone had children among the court. They'd reclaimed them and taken them home to begin the process of introducing them into a normal life in the real world.

It was still frustrating to be without those agents.

Of the seventy-five who initially pledged themselves to the cause of completely eliminating the Auditor organization, twelve more had already backed out. They were losing good agents daily.

Again, Tillie couldn't blame them.

Nicole had sent eight more away, despite their wish to remain and help, because they were too emotionally fragile.

That left them with just over fifty agents, to take down an ancient, powerful, international secret society.

Oh, but there were also the Catholics. Sister Catherine and her band of nuns were nothing to sneeze at, and they seemed to think there was a possibility that the Vatican would send more fighters to help out.

Tillie flipped to a new page, recording the strengths of the convent of the Sisters of Saint Joan.

Of course, the nuns were constrained by the red tape of the Church, and there was always the possibility that Rome would tell them to back off instead.

Even now, Sister Catherine was waiting for orders from the Vatican on what to do with the court prisoners taken in last week's battle, who were still languishing in the dungeons below their convent and school.

And the children taken from the court after the battle. Most of their parents were still agents of the Auditor organization. Some of them had been children of courtiers. All of them were confused and traumatized and were taking up a lot of the convent's time and resources as they waited for someone from the Church to come and deal with them.

And, of course, the nuns still had their regular duties to deal with, running a girls' high school, the same one that Ida Garveldi – another staunch ally and one who couldn't be discounted either – had attended as a teen. Granted, the school's summer vacation had just started, but Tillie understood that there was still lots to do during the off-season.

As far as Tillie could see, Sister Margaret's only duty was slaying evil, but the rest of the convent had other things to do, which seriously hampered their ability to help.

They'd had some local mages helping too, members of the Garaveldi family, mobilized by Ida and her nephew Giovani, the mage who had started all of this for Tillie by warning her that the Auditors were coming for her.

Once the battle was over, most of the Garaveldi mages went back to their regular lives. Giovani, of course, as the ringleader of their movement, was still involved, and nothing could keep Ida out of it, but the rest of them had basically just told them to call if things got sticky again.

A knock sounded on the door, sharply interrupting Tillie's train of thought.

She jumped up, spinning around to stare at the door, a hand pressed to her chest for a second before shaking herself back to reality.

She turned on her seer sight and then smiled with relief to see that it was Giovani standing out in the hall, fidgeting with his light brown tie.

Her eyes went from white back to their typical bright blue as she turned her seer sight off and she walked briskly toward the door and opened it.

"Hi," said Giovani.

Tillie stepped back as he drifted into the living room. "Is everything okay?" she asked, remembering what time it was.

Giovani paused in the middle of the room and adjusted the cuffs of his perfectly tailored beige suit, which he wore like a uniform. He must have had a closet full of them.

"Hi," he said again.

Despite his well-groomed appearance, Tillie could see signs of wear and tear on him – his ragged thumbnails in contrast to the manicured fingernails; an ever-so-slight shadow on his cheeks and chin; the minute tapping of his left foot as he stood awkwardly in front of her.

She closed the door and gave him a gentle smile. "Hi, Giovani. Why don't you sit down? I'll make some tea."

"Yes. Tea. Great. Thanks." Giovani wandered over to the couch, plopping down and closing his eyes.

Glad to have something to do, Tillie hurried into the kitchen to fill her electric kettle. She selected a soothing mint-flavored green tea, setting the temperature on the kettle accordingly. As she went about the familiar ritual of measuring out tea leaves and arranging a tray with honey, hand-thrown clay mugs, and some coconut macaroons, she wondered whether Giovani was going to be okay in the long run.

Tillie herself was no stranger to post-traumatic stress disorder and she recognized the signs in him, as well as in the rest of the former Auditor agents. As far as she was concerned, her own past paled in comparison to the ordeals they had been through, and it had taken her months after her divorce to feel like she was able to live a normal life again.

The kettle clicked off and Tillie reached for it, careful to grab the insulated handle as warmth radiated from the pitcher.

Would he ever be able to feel normal? To hold down a stable job? Be a good father to his son? Have a long-term relationship?

Tillie frowned at herself as she poured steaming water over the tea leaves. Best to steer clear of that line of thinking – it would only complicate everything even more than it already was. Giovani was too much her type and it had been longer than she was accustomed to going between lovers.

What was more, Giovani was both of her types. Tillie tended to like men who were creative and sensitive, which seemed to be Giovani's default personality. She suspected he would have been some kind of artist if things had gone differently.

But she had always been attracted to women who were tough and strong, exactly what his life had forged him into.

Giovani was the best of both worlds.

She shook her head. Enough of that. There were plenty of fish in the sea. Ones who had never been assigned to kidnap her. Ones who weren't in the middle of existential crises. Ones who she wasn't going to be working with on a mission that meant everything to both of them.

She picked up the tray, squared her shoulders, strengthened her resolve, and walked back into the living room, setting the tea things down on the coffee table. She sat down on the other end of the sofa and crossed her legs, suddenly very aware that she was wearing only a negligee.

Feeling uncharacteristically self-conscious, Tillie snagged a soft throw blanket from the basket beside the couch and draped it over her legs.

"Hi," said Giovani again.

"That's quite the vocabulary you've got this morning," said Tillie with a gentle smile. She picked up the remote and turned off the TV. The news had moved on to sports anyway.

"I'm sorry," said Giovani. "I'm sorry to barge in on you at this time of the day. I just – I had to – I couldn't – I'm so—"

"I know," said Tillie. "It's okay. You couldn't sleep? Neither could I."

"I was on guard duty at the building, midnight to four."

Tillie frowned. "They gave you the graveyard shift? I thought we agreed that the more stable people would be on the harder stints." She realized what she'd just said and lifted a hand to cover her mouth, embarrassed. "I'm sorry. I just meant—"

"It's okay." Giovani smiled wryly. "I assigned myself the graveyard shift. I can't seem to give myself a break. And Susan was originally supposed to be on it, but she left yesterday afternoon. So I guess she wasn't as stable as we thought."

Tillie's heart ached at his haunted eyes. She reached out and rested her hand on his arm. "You need a break, hon. Give yourself permission to be a human being."

"I'd rather be a robot," he admitted. "I feel better when I push myself. But only while I'm doing it. As soon as I have a moment of respite, that human fragility takes over, and I feel like crap. I couldn't face going home, knowing I won't sleep, just toss and turn."

He turned to face Tillie, and she found herself eyeing his lips, wondering what kind of a kisser he was.

She shook herself, hurriedly pulling her hand away and busying herself with the teapot instead. Seriously. This had to stop.

Tillie pulled out the strainer cup, placing it on a saucer, and began to pour the tea into the mugs. "I couldn't remember how you take your tea," she said. "It's green tea with mint, and I've got honey here, but if you take cream or sugar or agave or anything, I've got all of that in the kitchen. And there are some cookies here too. Trevor brought them over yesterday; they're from his favorite bakery, DiAngelo's, on the Hill."

"Honey is great," said Giovani. "Thank you."

Tillie forced herself to stop babbling, spooning sweetener into his mug and stirring to dissolve it, focusing on watching the thick amber honey disappear into the hot tea.

What the hell was wrong with her? She hadn't drooled over someone like this in years. She was an escort, for crying out loud.

Well, retired escort.

She handed Giovani his tea. As she swiveled back toward the coffee table to grab her own mug, the blanket fell to the ground, baring her lean legs once again.

Tillie abruptly stood. This was getting ridiculous. "I'm just going to go get changed," she said. "I'll be right back."

She strode into her room and quickly tossed on a pair of charcoal gray yoga pants and a slim-fitting black cotton t-shirt with a built-in sports bra.

When she returned, Giovani had fallen asleep on her couch.

Tillie smiled and gently arranged him in a more comfortable position, covering him with the discarded blanket.

She sipped her tea and regarded him for a moment, then returned to her bedroom to start her morning workout.

***

Whirling around, Mattie saw another woman kicking out toward Sister Margaret, her eyes as black as Steve's had been. Mattie recognized her as one of the rebel Auditors, a stitcher. One she didn't know very well at all.

Annie? No, Amy.

Amy kicked at Sister Margaret's wrist, but the seer pulled her arm back and reversed her grip on the swords, swinging with the hilts outward instead of the blades.

Mattie danced in place, looking for an opening into which she could charge as she had before. She made a mental note to not use her head as a weapon this time, although Sister Margaret was right – she was already in less pain.

Seeing her chance at last, Mattie bellowed and charged into the fray, wrestling Amy to the ground and pinning her down.

Amy rolled her over and sprang back up to her feet, just in time for Sister Margaret to nimbly spin, her arm swinging around, and smack Amy on the side of the head with her sword-hilt. The stitcher went limp.

"Come on," said Sister Margaret, extending a hand to Mattie. "We have to go."

As she pulled herself up, Mattie heard tires screeching and realized that their police friends had pulled a U-turn and drawn up beside them.

Their fight had moved them past her sight shield.

Cursing, Mattie extended the shield to where they now stood, her energy reserves draining to nearly empty.

Two officers leaped from the car, drawing their guns and looking around wildly.

"Where did they go?" shouted one.

"Drop your weapons and show yourselves!" yelled the other.

Sister Margaret gestured to the fallen stitcher and mimed picking her up.

Mattie nodded and silently grabbed her under the arms.

Sister Margaret took her legs, and they carried her toward the van.

With each step, Mattie's weariness grew.

Finally, they reached the side door.

She shook her head urgently, trying to convey that the sight shield didn't cover the van.

Her friend seemed to understand, as she gently lowered her half of the unconscious mage to the ground.

Mattie followed suit and turned her attention to Steve, their other unconscious captive. She took a deep breath, trying to find new reserves. A hand touched her arm, and she felt Sister Margaret channeling mage energy into her.

With a grateful smile, Mattie levitated Steve a couple inches off the ground and began moving him toward them. As she did so, she saw his eyes flutter open.

She drew in a sharp gasp, then let it go as she saw that his eyes looked ordinary once again.

He was also starting to move the fingers on his unbound hand.

Mattie reinstated the immobilization spell, and he froze mid-stitch, his face stuck in a glare. She resisted the urge to giggle, remembering how she'd loved to make silly faces as a child, and every adult ever had told her to knock it off or her face would freeze like that.

Hysteria was probably setting in if she was thinking about things like that at a time like this.

Got to stay focused. Eye on the prize.

Mattie worked on slowly, carefully, drawing him toward the van, navigating him over the uneven sidewalk and around the debris that always seemed to accumulate in a neighborhood like this.

She forced herself to ignore the cops as they continued to bark orders at them to show themselves.

Apartment-dwellers were starting to appear on balconies up and down the street, and she noticed out of the corner of her eye that the brewers in the building right next to them were peering out the window.

Mattie finally had Steve positioned where she wanted him, level with the van door, just on this side of the sight shield. She levitated Amy to the same height right beside him and nodded to Sister Margaret.

Sister Margaret nodded back and put one hand on the door handle. She waited a moment, presumably using her seer mode to find just the right second to move without catching anyone's attention too much.

After about three seconds, she flung the door open and Mattie shoved the two captives into the back of the van. She dropped the sight shield – it was pointless now – and dashed around to the other side of the vehicle as Sister Margaret slammed the door shut and hurled herself back into the driver's seat.

Mattie's ass just barely managed to hit the passenger seat before Sister Margaret peeled out, pedal to the floor. She scrambled to grab hold of the door, heaving it shut as they screeched off.

The van narrowly missed one of the police officers who were rushing out into the street to intercept them.

Sister Margaret let out a whoop of pure joy, a manic grin lighting up her face as she rounded the corner on two wheels.

Mattie grinned too and groped for her seat belt as the two prisoners crashed around behind her. Mattie took pity on them and suspended them in midair with a spell.

Glancing in her mirror to check her work, Mattie saw a police car behind them. "Shit. They must have called for backup. No way they got back in their car that fast."

"No problem," said Sister Margaret. "Grab hold of something."

Mattie reached up and held onto the handle on the roof of the van just before Sister Margaret twisted the wheel abruptly, hauling ass down an alley.

She jumped as they clipped the corner of a dumpster and kept going.

Mattie threw a spell back toward the car chasing them, snickering as it stalled and came to a sudden halt.

Sister Margaret slowed slightly, taking the corners more carefully and navigating them back out onto an actual street. She pulled into a parking garage with the Saint Louis University logo on its sign, and then into a spot marked *Guest*.

Mattie spelled an illusion onto the van, turning it blue. "Nice teamwork back there. What happens now?"

"Now, we wait it out," said Sister Margaret. "Get comfy. We're not moving until I'm sure those cops aren't looking for us anymore."

"You're going to get caught," said Steve. His voice was flat and factual. And he shouldn't have been able to talk through an immobilization spell.

Mattie twisted around and peered back at him.

The seats had been cleared out of the back of the van at some point in the past and cushiony padding lined the floor, walls, and ceiling.

Her levitation spell had also failed and Steve was kneeling in the middle of the floor, his black-flooded eyes staring sightlessly at her, his unbound hand once again moving into a stitching gesture.

"What the actual fuck?" she yelped. She readied a fireball spell, then hesitated. Maybe throwing fireballs inside a van wasn't a great idea.

Nothing had come of his stitch yet – he was probably having trouble because he only had one hand to work with. Or it could be that whatever made him immune to spells and sight also interfered with his own mage abilities.

She dismissed the spell and instead held up her own hands. She wasn't a natural stitcher, but she'd been working on it. She looked around, but there was nothing in the back of the van she could stitch at his head to knock him out again.

Maybe if she stitched him a few inches to the left, it would distract him until Sister Margaret could finish with whatever she was doing.

Mattie could see Sister Margaret out of the corner of her eye, opening up the center console of the van and busying herself with something she'd pulled out of it. Some kind of small tube?

Forcing herself to focus on her stitch, Mattie made her gesture and held her breath.

It worked! Steve blinked out and back in, about five inches from his original position.

And in his new position, his eyes had reverted back to normalcy.

Before Mattie could really process that, Sister Margaret blew a dart through her tube, hitting the Auditor agent in the neck.

His eyes closed again and he slumped against the cushioned side of the van.

Silence filled the van. Mattie looked at Sister Margaret, who was staring back at their captives, the blow-tube still held to her lips.

Finally, the nun turned her head and met Mattie's eyes, her expression worried. "Generally, I favor moving cautiously, but I think we'd better get back to the convent. This can't wait."

Mattie snorted. Sister Margaret was the least cautious seer she knew. She didn't disagree, though. "I still have a couple of hours on my guard shift. I'd better call in Tillie to cover me."

She texted Tillie as Sister Margaret pulled the van out of the garage and headed toward the nunnery.

They passed five police cars on the way, and none of the officers gave their newly-blue van a second glance.

***

Tillie poured the rest of her tea into a travel mug, left a note beside the still-sleeping Giovani, and headed out the door to take over for Mattie at the burnt-out headquarters. As she strode down the stairs, she called for a taxi, making sure she had plenty of cash first.

One of the drawbacks to being officially dead was that she could no longer use rideshare apps or credit cards. Everything had to be anonymous, and if she ever ran into anyone from her old life, she always had to pretend to be her twin sister.

It was incredibly tedious. But on the other hand, it had gotten the Auditors to stop chasing after her.

For the moment.

She suspected that if the court managed to pull together the shreds of their organization – and there were clearly still a lot of shreds left – they'd be even more eager to kill her.

Not even bother to try to kidnap her this time.

Oh, well, it kept life interesting, right? She started to whistle as she jumped the last half of the bottom flight of stairs, pushing through the double glass exit doors just as her yellow chariot pulled up to the building.

"Grand and Lindell, please," she told the driver cheerfully as she slid into the back seat.

"You got it, sweetheart." The rather scruffy-looking man started the meter.

"I'm not your sweetheart."

***

Two hours later, having handed off the prisoners and briefed Sister Catherine, Mattie was finally released.

Sister Catherine had been as rattled as they had and proposed that they call an emergency meeting, gathering everyone at the convent to discuss this new development. Then she'd looked at Mattie's exhausted face and insisted that she go home and get some rest.

"We'll meet back up at noon," she'd said.

Mattie had shaken her head vigorously. "I'm good. Let's get this thing figured out," she'd protested.

But Sister Catherine had been adamant. "This will give me a chance to do some research anyway, and ensure we can get in touch with everyone."

Reluctantly, Mattie had allowed Sister Margaret to give her a ride back to where she'd parked her bike and had headed home for a nap.

But as Mattie pulled up to her house, a scream shattered the early-morning quiet, a long shrill wail followed by a brief pause and then repeating, like a human car alarm.

She abandoned her bike, the gears scraping against the back of her calf in her haste, and left it lying on its side on the front lawn, frantically fumbling with her keys as she bolted up the two steps to the front porch.

She jammed the key into the lock and twisted it hard, fighting with the old lock, tugging savagely on the door handle and cursing.

Finally, the lock clicked open and she wrenched the door toward her and rushed inside, slamming it shut behind her.

The screaming stopped abruptly.

Mattie paused to listen and heard a dull thud followed by a grunt. Now someone was fighting.

It was coming from one of the bedrooms.

She skidded down the short hallway and threw open the door of her housemate Nicole's room, from which the sounds were emerging.

Stopping in the doorway, Mattie stared at the spectacle in front of her. "What the fresh hell is this?"

Nicole was suspended two feet in the air in the middle of the room, spinning like a top, her long brown hair fanned out around her head, her blue-pajama-clad arms and legs outstretched, her freckled face tightened as though she was concentrating really hard. Her eyes were squeezed shut and her lips twisted into a painful-looking grimace.

A panicked thought raced into Mattie's mind – what color would her eyes be if they were open?

Mattie's other housemate, Danielle, was darting around, periodically making a grab at Nicole's limbs and grunting as she was smacked in the face or arm for her troubles.

"I have . . . no . . . idea," panted Danielle. "I ran in here and she was just like that. I tried a spell to get her to stop, but it didn't work. I'm just trying to slow her down now, I guess."

Spells didn't work.

Her heart sank at the familiarity and she was now certain that Nicole's eyes would be pitch black when they opened.

Mattie hurried forward to help. Crouching, she watched Nicole's bare right foot and made a grab for it as it passed. It slipped out of her fingers, but at least she didn't get kicked. This wasn't anything like what the other two had done – maybe it wasn't the same thing.

It couldn't be. This was her friend!

She attempted to insert some levity into the situation. "If she starts spewing pea soup, I'm out of here."

Danielle danced back for a rest, leaning against the textured white plaster wall. "Honestly, if she keeps spinning like that, she's definitely going to start spewing something at some point."

Mattie stood up and dashed forward, inserting her entire body into the path of Nicole's arms and legs, bracing herself just before they hit.

Nicole didn't even slow down; she just shoved Mattie along. Mattie staggered around and around for two revolutions before she managed to stumble out of Nicole's path. "Well, that didn't work, and I'm going to have a shitload of bruises. What kind of spell did you try?"

"A barrier," said Danielle. "She just cut right through it. She did stop screaming, though."

Mattie's eyebrows rose as she watched her spinning housemate thoughtfully. "Right when you did the spell?"

"Yeah. And then she punched me in the face."

Nodding, Mattie watched Nicole spin. Something had to be done.

She and Sister Margaret had knocked out Steve and Amy and that had worked on them.

She really didn't want to hit Nicole in the head.

What about stitching? When she had stitched Steve's body to a new spot, his eyes had reverted.

Mattie focused on her fingers, curling them into a very particular position and then twitching them in an arcane gesture designed to move Nicole one foot over from her current position.

Nicole disappeared and reappeared, no longer spinning, a few inches above her bed. She hung motionless in the air for a split second as Mattie and Danielle held their breaths.

Then her eyes flew open and she dropped down, landing on the mattress, finally still, limbs sprawled.

Her eyes were pitch black.

Then, as Mattie inhaled sharply, Nicole's eyes snapped back to normal, her brown irises staring at them as she sat up groggily, leaving Mattie wondering if she'd just been projecting her worst expectations onto the situation – had she really seen the darkness there?

Mattie and Danielle rushed to Nicole's side. Mattie put an arm around Nicole's back, supporting her.

"What's going on? What are you guys doing in here?" asked Nicole, squinting at them both.

Mattie raised an eyebrow. "You don't remember?"

Nicole frowned. "I guess not. Remember what, exactly? Was I yelling or something? My throat is sore and I had the most awful dream."

"Was it that you were spinning around like the damn *Exorcist*?" asked Danielle, sitting down on

Nicole's twin bed and scooting back to lean against the wall, her long legs stretched out, crossing over Nicole's to dangle off the edge.

She was wearing an olive green t-shirt and plaid boxer shorts that hit her at mid-thigh and showed off legs fuzzy with a thick layer of dark blonde hair.

It felt odd to Mattie to see Danielle out of her usual cyberpunk vinyl gear and wearing something . . . normal.

"No.... Why? Did you have a dream like that?" Nicole pulled her own legs back, arranging herself in a cross-legged seat, leaning against the wall at the head of the bed.

Mattie looked around for another seat, but there was none, so she remained awkwardly standing.

"Not exactly," said Danielle. "What was your dream?"

"I was in Detroit. In the HQ where I trained when I was first brought in. The Pontiff was there, but younger, like the first time I saw him."

"You first saw the Pontiff while you were training?" said Danielle.

"No, not in real life. Just the dream. The first time I saw the court and the Pontiff wasn't until I got assigned to a station. I was a field agent for a couple of years before that." Nicole toyed with her tangled brown hair, working on undoing a gnarly knot. "In the dream, I was about halfway through my training, you know, at that point where you've bought in and you're trying to learn everything you can so you can be the best damn agent the organization has ever seen and atone for everything."

"Sure." Danielle nodded, the casual gesture belied by the haunted look in her eyes. Her breathing was a little bit ragged and she visibly pulled herself together before she started hyperventilating.

Mattie shivered. She couldn't begin to imagine the hell these women had been through, to say nothing of the strength it had taken to have pulled themselves out of it.

She felt vaguely guilty that her own life had been so relatively easy. She strengthened her resolve to take down the Auditors so no one else had to go through what they had.

"Well, in my dream, the Pontiff came and spoke to my class. There were six of us, just like in real life. The court wasn't there – just the Pontiff. And he . . . did something." Nicole's voice wavered. "Set some kind of spell on us."

Mattie met Danielle's eyes. "What kind of spell?"

Nicole shook her head. "I have no idea. I just know that while he was giving us a pep talk, his hands started glowing. And then they stopped."

"Then how do you know it was a spell on you?" said Mattie. "If they stopped glowing, then the spell was no longer in effect, right?"

"Or it went dormant," said Danielle grimly.

"I guess I just knew it," said Nicole. "Dream logic. I felt different somehow."

Danielle crawled closer to Nicole, gently pulling her hands from where they were still fiddling with her hair. "The Pontiff is dead. Any spell he set died with him." She sounded like she was trying to convince herself as much as Nicole.

Nicole nodded. "I know. It was just a dream."

"Was it, though?" asked Mattie. She tried to keep the frustration out of her voice. "You weren't just laying there dreaming, you know."

"What?" Nicole looked from Mattie to Danielle and back again.

Danielle quickly explained what they had walked into.

Nicole sighed, defeat written over every inch of her face.

"It gets worse," said Mattie. She told them about Steve and Amy. "Your eyes were that same horrible black, just for a moment, when you opened them," she finished. "Something seriously fucked is going on, and the absolute scariest part of it is that Sister Margaret and Sister Catherine are both freaked out about it too." She rubbed her forehead, wincing slightly as her finger hit the still-tender spot where she'd butted Steve. "We're meeting later today at the convent to discuss. I told them I'd pass it along to you."

Nicole nodded. "I'll mobilize the others." She sighed and closed her eyes, her head tilting back as she sagged against the wall.

Mattie studied her housemates. Both had dark circles under their eyes, their weariness made clear from their slouching postures and strained frowns. "In the meantime, let's all get some sleep."

2.

After three hours of guard duty, Tillie's cheer was greatly diminished by boredom.

Mattie had texted her again, asking her to stick around for a little extra time to cover for Nicole, who was having some kind of PTSD issue.

Of course, she was happy to help out, but that didn't mean she was happy to be just hanging around. Apparently, Mattie had gotten the full allotment of excitement for the day.

Glancing at her smartwatch, Tillie sighed. There was still an hour to go before she needed to leave for this emergency summit, which Mattie had also been very vague about.

She eyed a busy brewpub serving early brunch to day-drinking college kids across from the building, one of its patio tables newly abandoned. What would be the harm in having a pint of cider? Good camouflage, right?

She sat down at the vacant table and picked up the menu, grimacing as the plastic proved sticky with spilled beer. She moved her fingers minutely, stitching it clean, and studied it.

A cheerful young brunette woman approached, pulling a notepad out of her apron. "What can I get you?"

"Is the blueberry cider good?"

"Oh, yeah, it's my new favorite," the server assured her. "You waiting on anyone?"

"Just me today," said Tillie with a smile. "I'll take the blueberry."

"Anything to eat?"

"I don't think so."

Tillie watched the woman's shapely behind as she ambled off. Dammit, first Giovani and now her waitress? She needed to get laid. Stupid retirement.

Tillie eyed what little foot traffic there was, watching for anyone who looked like an Auditor. Actually, this was a fantastic idea – you were expected to be people-watching when you were sitting on a sidewalk patio alone.

Just then, someone slid into the seat opposite hers. So much for sitting alone.

She glanced over at the young man and groaned. "Sammy, what are you doing here?"

"What am I doing here?" He grinned. "I live across the street! I go to school right over there." He pointed up the street toward the university. "You're the one out of place here."

Tillie hadn't seen Sammy since the battle last Friday. Or to be more accurate, since just after the battle, when they'd stitched all of their people out of the burning HQ into his apartment building.

"Yes, well, you still shouldn't be here with me. You could get hurt." Tillie frowned as Sammy's smile grew wider. "I'm serious. You're not a mage."

He leaned forward. "I'd like to become one. How do I do that?"

Tillie sighed. She supposed that was a reasonable request. She'd been about his age when she'd discovered magery.

She hadn't jumped right into a battle, though.

But then again, she was a seer, and this kid was clearly a speller. Probably a pretty powerful one, considering just how impulsive he was. He was as bad as Mattie, actually. "Not by interfering with my mission."

"A mission, huh?" Sammy's eyes sparkled. "That sounds exciting. Do you work for the government or something? Are you, like, on some kind of magical task force?"

"Not even a little bit," said Tillie. "This is a self-imposed mission to take down an evil secret society."

His smile widened even further if that was possible. "Amazing," he breathed. "In actual fucking real life?"

She rubbed her temples, feeling a headache coming on. "Look, it's actually pretty tedious right now. I've been wandering around here for ages, just waiting for an enemy to show up. It's not all battles and excitement. It's work and ennui. And you're not prepared for the exciting stuff anyway."

"So teach me!"

"I don't have time!" she snapped. "I have a goddamn mission!"

Heads turned from the tables around them, and she lowered her voice. "I'm sorry. I just – I can't help you right now."

The server came back and set her cider down in front of her. "Here you are. One Blueberry Bonnet cider. Hi, Sammy. What can I get for you?"

"He's not staying," said Tillie firmly.

Sammy ignored her. "Hey, Carrie. I'll have the same."

"One more Blueberry Bonnet, coming up." She sauntered away.

"Seriously?" Tillie glared at Sammy.

He winked back at her. "This is my spot. I don't have to leave. You're free to leave. I'm not leaving. So, you don't have time to teach me magic. No problem. Who does? Who taught you?"

"A man named Tom French," she said absently. She spotted an oddly dressed woman walking down the sidewalk toward them. Tillie tried to watch the woman unobtrusively as she spoke. "He ran the massage school I went to after I—When I went to massage school. You could try there. Or Stephanie Bing, who runs Magpie Magic. She's a speller and she takes on apprentices now and then."

"What are you looking at?" Sammy began to turn around and Tillie kicked him under the table.

"Don't look!" she hissed. "Are you capable of being at all subtle, ever?"

"No, that's not really what I'm known for," he said cheerfully.

Tillie ignored him, eying the woman as she moved closer to their patio.

The newcomer seemed to be trying very hard to look casual. She wasn't dressed in the standard leather armor of an Auditor agent, but not all of them did.

Giovani had his beige suits. Danielle had her skintight black vinyl.

This woman was wearing a short red-and-white polka dot dress and had her hair and makeup done in a 1950s rockabilly style. Over the dress, she had a red belt at her waist and two red bandolier-style straps across her chest.

Looking closely, Tillie spotted a couple of well-hidden pockets that lay flat down the length of the straps – perfect for small daggers or stiletto knives.

Her feet were shod in red boots that came up to her mid-calf and didn't really go with the pin-up style of the rest of the ensemble, but which could definitely hold some weapons.

The dark-haired woman stopped and sat down on a bench a few feet away, looking at the burnt-out building thoughtfully and watching the police and firefighters coming in and out of its husk.

She didn't seem shocked to find the building in its current state, which could mean that she was one of theirs or it could mean that she was a seer or it could mean that she was unconnected to the organization altogether and had simply seen it on the news and come to check it out and was a little bit of an eccentric dresser.

Honestly, this neighborhood was full of eccentric dressers, which made Tillie's job that much harder.

Tillie watched and waited for any clue as to which scenario was most likely.

Carrie returned and set down Sammy's cider. "Can I get you two anything else?"

"We're good for now. Thanks, babe," said Sammy.

Tillie found herself distracted by Carrie's backside again as she walked away. "You know her?" she said to Sammy. "What's her deal?"

His eyebrows rose. "She just broke up with someone, actually. You want me to give her your number?"

Tillie's eyes slid back to the woman on the bench, who had just pulled out a cell phone. "No, no. I need to be focusing on the Auditors."

Sammy twisted around to look behind him again and Tillie let him this time. The woman's attention was on her phone anyway. "Is that lady an Auditor? Or another piece of ass you're eying?"

"An Auditor," said Tillie irritably. "Maybe. If she is, there should be another one around here—"

She broke off as she spotted someone who had to be the woman's partner, a man dressed in the same kind of retro outfit, in skinny jeans and a white t-shirt, complete with a pack of cigarettes rolled up in the sleeve. He was strolling just a little too casually on the other side of the street, pausing as he reached the yellow crime scene tape.

Something fell from his hand before he ambled onward, and Tillie automatically switched her seer sight on to see what it was, shading her eyes so no one at another table would notice.

"I don't know if I'll ever get used to that," she heard Sammy say as she zoomed in on the object.

It was a pen. She waited to see if it was going to do anything in the near future, but nothing happened.

Puzzled, she looked at the man who had dropped it and saw him joining up with the woman and the two of them walking away.

Tillie turned her seer sight off, frustrated at the lack of any concrete information. She sipped her cider without really tasting it as she watched the scene play out in real-time exactly the same way it had in her vision. She stood up. "I'll be right back. Don't drink my cider."

"I can help!" Sammy protested.

"Yes, you can help by saving my table," she called back over her shoulder as she followed the pair down the street. She slipped her teal Prada sunglasses off her head and over her eyes and then turned her seer sight back on, staying about ten feet back from the Auditor agents.

They turned down an alley and she saw them, in the superimposed future vision, setting an ambush for her. The woman pulled a dagger out of one of her boots and the man unrolled his sleeve to reveal that his pack of "cigarettes" was actually a set of darts, likely poisoned or at least drugged.

The woman's eyes were white, like Tillie's.

Tillie sighed. Fighting another seer was always frustrating, as neither could ever get ahead of the other. It only worked when one side outnumbered the other, and unfortunately, that scenario was against her in this case.

She weighed her options. She could attack anyway and hope that her ability to morph would give her an edge.

She played out this scene with her seer sight and saw herself outnumbered and taken captive.

She could—

Tillie's train of thought was interrupted by a voice floating toward her from the alley. "You're with Agent

Poe, then, are you?" The voice was female and had a faint British accent.

The other seer must have already done her own calculations.

"Nicole, yes," said Tillie. The future now showed the pair of apparently rogue agents coming back around the corner, shaking her hand, and heading back to the brewpub with her.

She relaxed and turned her seer sight off.

"Pleasure to meet you," said the woman, walking toward her. "I'm called Polly, and this is Bernie."

"Sorry about the ruse with the pen back there," said Bernie with a smile and a southern drawl. "We saw you watching, but weren't quite sure whose side you were on."

Tillie shook Bernie's extended hand. "Tillie. Totally understandable."

Polly's eyebrows shot up. "Tillie Holiday? Your reputation precedes you. A pleasure indeed. And now how about a pint?"

As they approached the patio, Tillie eyed the two empty glasses on the table. "I thought I said not to drink my cider," she said as she slid back onto her bench.

"Mine was empty," Sammy said with no sign of remorse. "I ordered you a new one."

As Bernie sat down beside Tillie, Sammy eyed him with interest. "Well, hello there."

"Hands off, little boy," growled Polly. "This one's taken."

"Honestly, have you ever met a man and not tried to hit on him?" asked Tillie. "You are ridiculous."

Sammy grinned. "I just have a lot of love to give," he said.

Carrie hurried up with two more ciders. "Wow, for someone who wasn't expecting anyone else, your table sure has filled up," she said with a smile. "What can I get for the two of you?"

Bernie and Polly ordered beers and Carrie left.

"Now," said Polly. "Let's talk rebellion. We were so sorry we couldn't make it out here for the battle last week."

Tillie noticed more odd glances toward their table, and she muttered a spell under her breath, putting up an aural shield around them.

Polly and Bernie exchanged an uneasy glance.

Tillie narrowed her eyes. "Is there a problem?" she asked coldly.

"Sorry," said Polly. "Just not used to it yet."

Sammy propped his chin up on his hands. "Used to what? What's going on now?"

"The whole morphing thing," she said.

"What's morphing?"

"Okay, that's it." Tillie stood up and walked around the table. She grabbed Sammy's arm and hauled him up. "I told you, I don't have time to train you. I don't have time to answer all of your questions. I don't have time for you to be here. I'm sorry if that's harsh. But this is life or death and you could get yourself killed. Or worse. You could get me killed."

"I don't really think that's worse," he muttered. He pulled his arm free and drew himself up to his full height, a not-very-impressive five-five. "Fine. I'll get myself trained up and then I'll find you and I'll show you just how helpful I can be."

"That sounds great," said Tillie.

"You've got the drinks, then?"

"Absolutely."

"Fine." He turned to go and then spun back around on his heel. "But if you think I'm going to help you get into Carrie's pants—"

"I can handle that all on my own," said Tillie through gritted teeth, extra glad she'd put up that sound shield, especially as she could see Carrie nearby, taking someone else's order.

Sammy nodded curtly and stalked off.

Tillie sat down again. "I'm sorry about that."

Polly laughed. "Is he your apprentice?"

"He wishes," said Tillie. "No, he's just someone who was in the right place at the wrong time."

"Right," said Polly. "So. How's everything going?"

"Oh, you know." Tillie sighed. "We're understaffed, broke, and overwhelmed."

Bernie leaned forward. "We're here to help with that middle thing."

Tillie perked up. "How?"

"Well," said Polly, reaching across the table to grab Bernie's hand. "This guy here is a tech genius. And they had him in charge of the finances for the Chicago HQ."

"So, last week, when Nicole told Polly here what y'all were planning, I started siphoning things off," said Bernie. "Moving Chicago's money into St. Louis' accounts, which is how y'all have been getting lodging and whatnot so quickly."

"Sure, but that went fast," said Tillie. She sipped her cider. It was very good – sweet with a tart bite right at the end. She took another sip.

Bernie grinned. "That's why I hacked into accounts all over North America and sent it into the St. Louis account. And then I locked that account up so only me and Nicole can get into it now."

"Really?" Tillie grinned. "So not only are we rich, but the organization is now broke, at least on this continent?"

"Exactly. And there's more."

"You're really going to like this one," Polly laughed.

"I got into the Cayman account," said Bernie triumphantly. "It wasn't easy, but I did it."

"The organization has an account in the Caymans?" Tillie's eyebrows shot up.

"A big one," said Polly. "All the extra money from all over the world goes in there or to Monaco. We're still working on Monaco."

Tillie's phone chirped and she pulled it out of her cross-body bag. "Sorry, it's my sister."

She read the text, which asked if she knew where Giovani was. Apparently, Mattie had been trying to reach him. She responded that he was asleep in her condo and tucked the phone away.

Before she could set her purse back down, another text came in. *How's patrol going? We have a little bit of a situation here and we're moving up the meeting to right now.*

Tillie frowned. That was hardly illuminating. Her twin used the term "situation" to mean anything from too-hot pizza to actual murder. *What kind of situation? I have a couple of new friends here and am briefing them.*

"Is everything all right?" asked Polly.

"Unclear," said Tillie.

The phone began to actually ring, a tinkly little tune playing.

Mattie's face smirked at her from the screen, an old photo that usually made Tillie smile – it had been taken their senior year of high school, on senior prank day, and Mattie had just finished spray painting a limerick about the principal on the side of the gym. A streak of blue paint decorated her cheek.

Today, a wave of worry washed over Tillie. Mattie wasn't one to call when a text would do. She swiped up to answer and held the phone up to her ear. "What's going on?"

"When you say 'new friends…'" said Mattie.

"Two rogue Auditor agents. Polly and Bernie. Apparently, Bernie is—"

"They aren't doing anything weird, are they?" Mattie interrupted. "What do their eyes look like?"

"Eyes? What are you talking about?"

"Thank goodness. Look, you've got to bring them in. Something's happening. You can't be alone with any of these people, at least not until we've figured out a way to scan them or something." Mattie's voice squeaked slightly in panic. "Bring them to the convent. They're all going crazy."

3.

Mattie hung up the phone and raked her fingers through her long red hair, pacing restlessly around the small waiting room outside the convent dungeon. Well, they called it a dungeon, but it wasn't what she thought of as a dungeon.

Which was good, actually, since they had started putting their friends in there.

She glanced through the plexiglass wall that divided her from the cell Nicole and Danielle were currently occupying.

Nicole looked up from her book and gave Mattie a tight smile. Mattie tried to smile back, but she could feel it going completely crooked.

Past the window to Nicole and Danielle's cell, she could see the hallway that stretched out for ages, cell after cell after cell, all of which contained friends or at least allies.

Dungeons shouldn't have friends in them.

But all morning, the rebel agents had started attacking each other or other mages with no provocation and no warning except for their eyes going completely black.

So, Nicole had suggested that they be locked up. Who could argue with that? After all, she herself was one of the detainees.

And she was counting on Mattie and the others to figure out what to do.

And at least these cells were nicer than the ones the actual Auditor agents and court were in, around the corner. This was the minimum security section apparently, although it wasn't clear to Mattie why they all had these giant windows that looked out into the hallway.

Giovani was the last one who needed to be locked up.

Well, and these two new agents Tillie had found.

Mattie scrolled through her contacts and texted Sister Margaret. *Giovani is at Tillie's condo. I guess he went over there after his guard duty and fell asleep.*

Address? Came the return text.

Mattie typed in her sister's address and sent it.

Then, with a final, sad glance toward her friends, she headed up the stairs and out through the secret door that led into the high school via a broom closet in the basement.

She wandered the lower level of the school.

Trevor had told her they'd be meeting in a classroom, but she couldn't remember what number he'd said.

All of the rooms on this floor seemed to be science labs and were empty, so she climbed another flight of stairs to the ground floor.

The first room she poked her head into contained Trevor and Father Sean busily rearranging the desks, pushing half of them against the wall and moving the remaining seats into rows.

Mattie hurried forward to take over for Father Sean, who had a pronounced limp and was struggling to carry the desk/chair combos.

"Sit down," she said. "I've got this."

He gave her a grateful smile and limped over to a desk toward the front of the room. "Thanks, dear. I don't get around like I used to."

Trevor gave her a warm smile. "Did you get it all figured out, Matts?"

"Yeah," she said. "Sister Margaret's bringing Giovani, and Tillie's on her way. She's bringing in two new ones."

"I think I've got an idea about how to detect the spells that are on the former Auditors," said Father Sean. "Of course, we won't be able to remove them without finding the speller who cast them."

"Or spellers," Trevor pointed out.

"What?" Mattie frowned at him as she shoved another desk across the tile floor with an abrasive squeal.

"I have a theory," he said. "It doesn't make sense to me that only these particular agents were spelled. I bet all Auditor agents get turned into sleeper agents during their training. I think each of them must have been spelled by someone stationed at the particular site where they were trained."

Mattie groaned. "Way to make everything so much more fucking complicated!"

Trevor smiled and slung a dark brown arm over her shoulders, giving her a gentle squeeze. "I'd hate for you to get bored."

"I love being bored," she said. "Boredom is my absolute preference."

"I don't believe that for a second," laughed Father Sean. "Never met a speller who wanted to be bored. Or a seer, for that matter. Only stitchers like the settled-in life."

"That checks out," said Trevor, raising an eyebrow at her. "I prefer boredom. You don't."

"I'm gonna, going forward," Mattie retorted. "And I have been doing a fair amount of stitching lately. Didn't Giovani say that morphing messes with your natural temperament?"

"I've heard that too," said Father Sean. "Part of why I never wanted to do it. Spelling is good enough for me, and I don't want to lose my edge."

Mattie cocked her head as a thought occurred to her. "Are Church mages allowed to morph?"

Father Sean shrugged. "I've heard of it. We've never had to worry about the Auditors, I guess, being under the Church's protection. I overheard Sister Catherine talking about introducing it to the curriculum now that it's all out in the open, though. You're going to teach here, right? Maybe she wants you to teach morphing. Don't know anyone else around here who could."

"I get to teach magic?" Mattie dropped the desk she was carrying with a thud, her face breaking into a grin. "That sounds like so much fun!"

"Maybe I misspoke," said Father Sean. "I don't know if Sister Catherine has you in mind for magery courses, but all of the Catholic schools around here do teach it. They call it 'Latin class' to weed out the ones from non-mage families. Because who the hell would actually want to take Latin?"

Sister Catherine walked into the room just then, and Mattie pounced on her. "Will I get to teach magery classes?"

Her new boss smiled. "If you'd like. I think you'd be an asset to our Latin department, especially since you practice multiple disciplines. Once you've got a bit more experience, of course."

Mattie grinned. "Well, the way this summer is going so far, I'll get plenty of practice by the time school starts back up."

Sister Catherine nodded, but she looked a little bit less enthused.

Two more nuns walked in and took seats, followed by another man in the off-duty priest uniform of blue jeans, black shirt, and dog collar.

Mattie looked around and decided that was enough desks. Their group was pretty much decimated by the absence of the rebel Auditor agents.

She sat down too.

Sister Catherine strode to the front of the room. "Is this everyone? This can't be everyone. Where is Sister Margaret? And Sister Timothy Ann? Does anyone know if Ida Garavelli will be here?"

"Sister Margaret is picking up Giovani from Tillie's condo," said Mattie.

"Sister Tim is on her way up," said one of the other nuns, a frail-looking blonde woman who wore a wimple that was always somewhat askew.

Mattie couldn't remember her name.

"And Tillie is also on her way," said Trevor. "She'll have to check in the two new people first."

Sister Catherine nodded. "We'll wait, then. For Tillie and Sister Tim at the very least. Has anyone heard from Ida?"

Tillie sauntered in just then, choosing a seat next to Trevor. "Am I late?" she asked, brushing back a lock of her short, red hair from her forehead. She was growing it out so that she and Mattie would look more identical, but at this point, it was only a little bit longer than her usual pixie cut.

"No, we're just—" began Sister Catherine. She was interrupted by a cacophony of phone alerts throughout the room.

Everyone pulled out their cell phones from pockets or purses, frowning down at a group text sent by Sister Margaret. *Giovani is not at Tillie's condo. He seems to be missing. Please advise.*

The room erupted as everyone started talking at once, spellers jumping to their feet to shout and argue, while stitchers tried to calm the room and seers flipped their eyes into white mode to see what they could see.

"Enough!" came a tired voice from the doorway. The voice still held enough authority to cut through the din, despite the weariness apparent in it. "Quiet down!"

Ida Garaveldi made her way to the front of the room, her steps slower than they usually were, her knees wobbling slightly as she walked. She stood before them, her hands resting on a chair in front of her, thick iron-grey eyebrows high on her forehead as she waited for the residual muttering to subside. "One person speaking at a time is the most efficient way to hold a meeting, I always say," she admonished them. "Now, someone tell me what is going on."

Mattie sat down as three people tried to respond to Ida at once.

Ida clapped her hands once and everybody shut up again. She pointed to Trevor. "You. What is going on?"

"Are you aware of the situation with the Auditor agents?" he asked.

"Former Auditors, I assume you mean," she said. "I heard they're under some kind of spell. They're attacking each other?"

"Right." Trevor nodded. "Well, we've rounded up all the ones we have, on their own insistence, and set them up in the dungeons downstairs."

Ida tsked. "That's a damn shame, but I'm glad they went willingly. It's easier to deal with a problem when everyone's on board with actually dealing with it, I always say. Sometimes you just have to do what you have to do, I suppose."

"Sure," said Trevor. "But we're one short." He paused and Mattie felt a little bit sorry for him to have to deliver the news to Ida. Ida was very protective of her own family, and Giovani was her nephew.

"Who's that?" asked Ida.

Trevor bit his lip.

"It must be my wayward nephew, I suppose, from the way you're prevaricating," said Ida. "Is it Giovani?"

"Yes, ma'am," said Trevor meekly.

"The little bastard is always disappearing," Ida sighed.

Mattie burst out laughing. She couldn't help it. She clapped her hands over her lips, as everyone in the room turned to stare at her.

From the front of the room, Ida's rich, comfortable laugh rang out too, and Mattie relaxed. She dropped her hands and grinned at the old woman. You could always count on Ida not to take things too seriously.

"Well, let's see here," said Ida. "I'm no good at coming up with plans. Let's get a seer up here."

Sister Crooked Wimple stood up and made her way to the head of the classroom.

Ida took a seat in the front row, next to Father Sean.

"There are two situations that need addressing here," she began. Her voice was high and flutelike, almost piccoloesque. "We need a plan to deal with the spell placed on our allies downstairs so that they can go back to being true allies. And we need to find Giovani and bring him in to join his compatriots."

Sister Timothy Ann slipped into the room and took a seat in the back.

Another nun raised a hand. "I think the question regarding Giovani needs to be whether he's lost or has actually doubled back to being against us once again."

"Giovani saved my life," snapped Tillie. "He is loyal to our cause. Hell, he started this cause!"

The nun lifted her hands, palms out in a placating way. "I'm not suggesting that his loyalty has shifted. I'm wondering if the spell has driven him back into the arms of the organization."

"As unpleasant as that idea is, it needs to be considered, I suppose," said Ida.

"All I'm saying is that we would be looking in different places depending on what the actual scenario is," said the nun. She looked young, in her twenties, but wore a full floor-length navy blue habit and a wimple that completely covered her hair.

Mattie wondered why. Most of the sisters under forty seemed content to wear regular clothes and only a few of them even wore the head covering.

"An excellent point, Sister Helen," said Sister Catherine. She addressed Ida. "You know him best. What do you think is most likely?"

Ida threw her hands in the air. "I knew him a little when he was a child and a little less when he was a young man. I don't know him at all now. Tillie seems to be spending a good deal of time with him lately. We should ask her, I suppose."

All eyes in the room turned toward Tillie, who looked slightly flustered.

Mattie's lips twitched. She hadn't seen Tillie looking quite so awkward since they were teens. Was she – she *was* blushing!

Mattie's eyes met Trevor's, and she saw amusement written across his face as well.

"I know he was having trouble sleeping last night," Tillie began.

Mattie cleared her throat to quash the laugh bubbling back up.

Tillie looked at her and narrowed her eyes.

"How do you know that?" Mattie asked, innocently.

"He showed up at my door this morning," said Tillie, a note of defensiveness in her voice, her eyes narrowing. "He said he'd been on guard duty and didn't want to go home, because he hadn't been able to sleep anyway, and he was feeling restless or something. I don't remember exactly what he said. But I let him in and made some tea and he fell asleep on my couch and then Mattie texted me to cover for her on guard duty, so I left him a note and that was the last time I saw him."

Tillie leaned back in her seat and crossed her arms over her chest, her lips forming a thin line. Clearly, that was all she was going to say.

Mattie smothered another smile.

The door crashed open, slamming against the wall as Sister Margaret marched into the room and right up to the front. "Well?" she said. "What's the plan?" She danced in place, clearly ready to get back out there. "No one responded to my text. I sent a text to literally all of you, and not one of you motherfuckers responded."

"We're still talking it over," said Sister Catherine. She put a hand on Sister Margaret's arm and guided her to a seat.

Sister Margaret sat down for a split second and then bounced back to her feet. "Nope! Can't sit down! Too fired up! We've gotta find this guy!" She began pacing the aisle.

Mattie sympathized. She was eager to get back to action too. The organization wasn't going to destroy itself, after all.

"Why don't you tell us what happened at Tillie's condo?" suggested Trevor. "Was there any sign that Giovani had gone rogue? Anything he left behind? Any clues at all?"

She shrugged. "I got to the building and buzzed up, but no one answered. I know another mage who lives in that building, so I texted her to let me in, and when I got up to Tillie's condo, I knocked. Again, there was no answer, so I picked the lock. The place was empty. I searched the whole apartment, and there was no one there. I did see Tillie's note. It was on the floor in the living room. But no other sign that Giovani was ever there."

The room was quiet for a moment, as everyone pondered her words.

"Has anyone tried texting Giovani?" asked Trevor.

More silence, as no one came forward.

Mattie picked up her phone from the desk in front of her, where she'd dropped it. She typed in a quick text. *Please come to St. Elizabeth Academy as soon as you can.* "I have now," she said.

Another long pause ensued, as everyone waited for the return text.

"This is ridiculous," said Father Sean. "Why don't you call him?"

"Because it never occurs to me to call people," said Mattie. "It feels rude. The only person I call is my ex-husband. I don't mind being rude to him."

"We can be rude, just this once, I suppose," said Ida. "Ask forgiveness later, I always say, although in my day calling was the default. All of this texting and twittering nonsense is just a waste of time, I always say."

Mattie hit the phone icon in the corner of the text app and put it on speaker mode so everyone could hear. It rang.

And then rang again.

And then went to voicemail.

She hung up.

"You're not going to leave a message?" said Father Sean.

Mattie shrugged. "I already texted him. Leaving a voicemail seems redundant."

"Okay, well, either he's not interested in chatting or he can't get to his phone, I suppose. No point in dwelling, I always say," said Ida. "Let's move on to finding him."

"Based on the number of rings, I'm guessing he's not interested in chatting," remarked Trevor. "He clearly sent it to voicemail."

"Does it matter?" asked Mattie.

"Yes," said Tillie. "If he is ignoring us, that's a completely different scenario and will require a completely different plan than if he's in trouble and can't answer."

"Okay, so let's assume he's turned back to being the enemy," said Sister Margaret with a little too much relish. "How do we crush him?"

Sister Catherine leveled an admonishing look at her. "I think you mean, 'How do we bring him in so that we can undo the spell he's under?'"

Sister Margaret waved one hand, finally plopping down into a chair. "Yeah, sure, whatever. What's the next step?"

"He still could have sent it to voicemail because answering isn't an option because he's in a sticky predicament," Tillie protested. "It doesn't mean he's ignoring the call."

Sister Margaret shrugged. "Either way, my recommendation is to start with his last known location, which was Tillie's condo. Maybe he's still in the neighborhood. Or even the building."

"The general pattern behind this spell has been that they're only black-eyed for about five to fifteen minutes," said Trevor. "Then they snap out of it with no memory of what happened."

"Which makes it unlikely that he's hiding out!" said Tillie.

"Then why isn't he answering his phone, chica?" said Sister Margaret. She pulled out a small dagger and used it to clean under one of her fingernails.

"Okay, now we're just going around in circles," said Mattie. She smacked a hand on the desk in front of her for emphasis. "I vote we break into teams. One team goes to look for Giovani. One team stays here to crack the code of this attacking spell."

"Yes," said Sister Helen. "That makes sense. Let's do that."

"All right," said Ida. "Let's get to it, then." She began pointing at people one by one. "You, you, you, and you. You're on spell-cracking duty with me. The rest of you, go find my nephew, and try not to hurt him too much."

Sister Crooked Wimple lifted a finger and opened her mouth as though to object, but Ida crossed her arms and glared. "Just go," she ordered, nodding toward the door.

Sister Crooked Wimple shrugged and strode out the door, snagging Father Sean by the arm as she went. Father Sean took a few limping steps and then levitated himself a couple inches off the ground, letting the nun drag him along.

Mattie was in the spell-cracking group, which suited her fine. As long as she was doing *something* to get this shit taken care of.

She jerked her head at Trevor and they followed Father Sean and Sister Crooked Wimple out and down the hall.

She was really going to have to learn Sister Crooked Wimple's name.

4.

Tillie found herself riding to her condo in the back seat of a green Ford Fiesta with Sister Timothy Ann and a kind-faced priest who introduced himself as Father Bruce. The name suited him and his stocky, barrel-like build.

The car smelled faintly of chicken noodle soup.

The ride got off to a rocky start, as Sister Timothy immediately asked, "So, Tillie. What do you do for a living?"

Tillie paused, considering her options. "I'm retired, actually," she said carefully. "Sort of. Technically I'm legally dead. So I was forced into early retirement."

"Fascinating!" said Father Bruce. "How did that happen?"

Grateful that she had managed to steer the conversation in a new direction, Tillie recounted the events that had led to her faked death – Giovani warning her that the Auditors were after her, their pursuit of her across the country, Mattie and Trevor coming to her rescue and helping her fight them off.

"Wow," breathed Sister Timothy, regarding her in the rear-view mirror. "No wonder you're so quick to defend Giovani. He did save your life."

"And in a way, we have you to thank for our current quest," observed Father Bruce.

Tillie tensed. She hadn't meant to drag the clergy into this whole mess. Was he pleased or upset to be here?

"Yes," agreed Sister Timothy. "Thank you for helping us to recognize the threat of this shadowy organization that we could eradicate its evil from God's earth."

That just made Tillie even more tense. Why did they have to bring religion into it?

"Anyway," said Father Bruce. "I don't think you said what you were retired from?"

Tillie's neck and jaw began to ache with the tension. "I worked for . . . an agency . . . that supplied . . . companionship. For people who . . . needed companionship."

"Like the elderly?" said Sister Timothy. "Were you some kind of home healthcare worker?"

"Not exactly," she said. Maybe she should just lie. Tillie was not in the habit of lying, nor was she in the habit of being ashamed of her profession. If anything, she tended to enjoy the discomfort of prudish people when she told them what she did.

But these two were so nice, and what was more, they seemed like genuinely good people, which didn't always go hand-in-hand with niceness and especially didn't always go hand-in-hand with the deeply religious, in her experience.

She opened her mouth to say something about working with mentally ill children or something.

"I think she means she was an escort," said Father Bruce.

Tillie's mouth snapped shut.

There was no judgment in the priest's voice whatsoever.

"Oh, of course, how silly of me!" said Sister Timothy with a small self-deprecating laugh. "Which agency were you with?"

"What?" said Tillie weakly.

"I'm just curious. Father, what is the name of that charming young lady who volunteers at the food pantry on Wednesdays?"

"Elena," he said. "Elena Rose, I believe."

"Do you know Elena?" Sister Timothy's eyes met Tillie's in the mirror again.

"Um." Tillie cleared her throat. "Yes, actually, I do. She doesn't work for the same agency I did. But you pretty much get to know everyone on the same echelon as you. You end up at all the same parties, you know."

"Well, that makes perfect sense, of course," said Sister Timothy. "I take it I shouldn't mention you to her, however? Since you're dead?"

"I'd appreciate it." Tillie's jaw finally began to unclench.

***

Mattie slipped into Nicole and Danielle's cell to find Nicole sleeping in the bottom bunk and Danielle sprawled on a loveseat, reading something on her phone.

One of Danielle's eyes was surrounded by a large bruise.

"What happened?" Mattie hurried to her friend's side, studying the injury.

"Oh, you know," said Danielle, her voice weary. "Nicole's eyes went black and she started punching me. I tried to put up a shield, but just like this morning, she just punched right through it. I didn't want to hurt her, so I picked up a couch cushion and used it to absorb her blows. She wasn't as good a fighter as she usually is, so I just waited it out. In the meantime, she gave me this shiner."

Mattie grimaced. "Maybe we should have given everyone their own cell."

"Pretty sure solitary confinement is considered torture in most countries," said Trevor from the doorway.

"It's not exactly the same," Mattie protested. "These are pretty comfy cells and they still have their phones. They can still communicate with each other and with the outside world. They just wouldn't be able to punch each other."

Trevor gently pushed Mattie aside and knelt in front of Danielle to examine her black eye.

Mattie stepped over to the small table against the wall and plopped herself into one of the two chairs beside it, leaning against one elbow on the table.

Trevor made an arcane gesture, and the bruise was gone. "Can you tell us exactly what happened?" he asked. "The more information we have about this spell, the better equipped we'll be to shut it down." He addressed Mattie. "Another reason to keep them in pairs – this way there's always a witness."

"And we don't even know if the spell would be triggered at all without someone around to attack," Danielle pointed out. "The only time that's happened so far, it was a stitcher and she stitched to the nearest ally to attack them."

"Yes," said Mattie dryly. "I was, in fact, the nearest ally when that happened."

"Right," said Danielle. "Sorry."

"This latest event?" Trevor reminded them. "What happened there?"

"Maybe we should wait for the others," said Mattie.

"Who else is coming?" asked Danielle.

"We've got a team put together to start figuring this shit out," said Mattie. "Us, Ida, Father Sean, and some nun I don't know."

"Sister Regina," said Trevor. "She's a seer, I think. The others are just gathering some supplies."

"Okay, well—" Danielle began. Suddenly, mid-word, her eyes filled with inky blackness and she jumped to her feet, fists swinging toward Trevor.

Mattie leaped up too, shoving Trevor out of the way and crossing her arms protectively in front of her face to deflect Danielle's strikes. "Trevor!" she yelled. "Can you stitch her into a new position?"

Danielle disappeared from where she was, reappearing a split second later across the cell, her eyes back to human. She dropped her arms. "Fuck! Did it just happen to me? Are you guys okay?"

"Yeah, we're fine," said Mattie. "We stitched you and you stopped."

Danielle frowned as she moved back to her loveseat and sank down into it. "Why does that work? It doesn't make any sense."

Nicole sat up on her bunk. "What's going on?" she asked, standing and stretching.

"We're going to save you," said Mattie.

"Hopefully," corrected Trevor, gently. "Father Sean has an idea."

Ida, Father Sean, and Sister Regina appeared in the doorway, carrying an assortment of esoteric supplies.

"Is everything okay in here?" said Father Sean.

Mattie recounted the events of the last few minutes.

"So, if we can't figure out what's going on, we can make sure to always have a stitcher on hand," Sister Regina suggested. "To disrupt it as quickly as possible."

"Unless it's the stitcher who's attacking," Mattie pointed out. "What is all that stuff?"

Sister Regina set down a clear crystal about the size of Mattie's fist on the table. "My scrying stone, so I can see what's going on in their energy systems." She gestured for Ida and Father Sean to set down a black crystal obelisk, a piece of white poster board, and a bag of popcorn. "The pointy one helps to focus our energy while we're working together. The poster board is so a speller can project what I'm seeing onto it for everyone to see. If the spell is affecting the meridians, a stitcher can sometimes at least partially correct that."

Mattie frowned. "Affecting the what?"

"Meridians are the lines that connect chakras, right?" said Trevor. "Like in eastern medicine?"

"Seriously?" said Mattie. "You believe in all that hippy shit?"

Sister Regina glared at Mattie. "Yes, like in eastern medicine. And it's not hippy shit."

"I get where you're coming from, Mattie," said Ida, her eyes sparkling, "But magery and energy healing are closely related, and if you're going to believe in one, you'll have to start believing in the other, I'm afraid."

Mattie lifted her hands in surrender. "Okay, fine. We'll try the hippy shit."

"Thanks for your permission," said Sister Regina shortly.

"And the popcorn?" asked Danielle. "What's that for?"

"We might be here for a while," said Sister Regina. "I get nauseous if I don't eat."

"Well, the sooner we get started, the sooner we'll get finished, I always say," said Ida. "What do you need from us?"

Sister Regina turned to Mattie. "I understand you use multiple disciplines?"

"I'm a speller and I'm learning to stitch too," she replied.

The nun's eyebrows raised. "Not to see?"

"I haven't tried," said Mattie.

"She's really powerful," put in Danielle. "I'm sure she can see if she puts her mind to it."

"But isn't it a physical trait that lets you change your eyes?" said Mattie. "How can I do that if I wasn't born a seer?"

"You're overthinking it," said Sister Regina. "Which isn't a problem spellers usually have, frankly, which tells me that you have been stitching, and it's probably been coming pretty naturally to you, right?"

"It doesn't feel natural." Mattie frowned, not sure if she was being insulted or complimented. She decided to take the advice to heart and stop overthinking. "But I have been practicing a lot."

"Okay," said Sister Regina. "Well, I need you to try seeing, because the teams were chosen by a speller, who didn't think things through, which isn't her fault –

that's just what spellers do – and now we're stuck with three spellers and only one stitcher and one seer. So I need you to help with the stitching and the seeing."

"Excuse me?" Ida snapped.

Mattie had to admire Sister Regina's courage as she faced down Ida. Maybe she wasn't as delicate as she looked.

"There were three seers in that room," Sister Regina pointed out. "I'm the only one you assigned to this team."

Ida crossed her arms. "You expected me to send a team to Tillie's condo without sending Tillie with them?"

"Sister Margaret could have been a valuable asset to this task!" said Sister Regina.

Mattie snorted. "If you think Sister Margaret was going to stay here and do hippy shit when there was an option to tear the city apart hunting down a renegade, you don't know her at all."

Sister Regina narrowed her eyes. "Well, the fact remains that we have only one natural seer."

Ida opened her mouth, but before she could rebut, Trevor restrained her with a gentle arm, giving her a wry smile and murmuring, "She's kind of bitchy, but she's not wrong."

Ida rolled her eyes but subsided.

Sister Regina smiled smugly and gestured to Mattie to sit down.

"It's okay, Ida," Mattie added. "I've been wishing I could see anyway. I want to learn." She sat on a chair and waited for instructions.

"Now," said Sister Regina. "I want you to relax your face."

"Okay." Mattie forced her facial muscles to slacken. Her eyes started to close and her mouth opened slightly.

"Keep your eyes from closing all the way."

She allowed her eyelids to drift back open.

"Good." Sister Regina nodded. "Now look into the future."

Mattie's brain stumbled. How was she supposed to do that? Wasn't Sister Regina supposed to be guiding her into how to —

Suddenly, she could see the future overlaid onto the present. Everyone in the room multiplied, and somehow she knew exactly which figures represented the present and which were doing what they were going to do in two seconds, and there was even a third set of figures doing what they were going to do in four seconds, and it was all extremely overwhelming.

She yelped and jumped to her feet, her face tensing up.

The future disappeared.

"Good!" Sister Regina clapped her on the shoulder and she staggered forward. "Now do it again and this time don't freak out about it."

***

Tillie led the way up the stairs to her second-floor condo, where Sisters Catherine, Helen, and Margaret already waited in the hall.

"How did you get into the building?" she raised an eyebrow. "Your friend again?"

"No, I took the liberty of stitching us in," said Sister Catherine. "Honestly, you'd think a building full of mages would have shields against that."

Tillie shrugged. "It's actually a pretty chill building. No drama. Most of the people living here picked it because they like the no-drama thing. It's not meant to be a fortress, like some of the other mage enclaves in town."

Sister Catherine raised an eyebrow. "Well, I was glad to see that you, at least, have shields on your own door against stitches."

Tillie frowned. "I do? I didn't put those up."

She moved her fingers into a pattern designed to put herself on the other side of her door. Nothing happened. She tried again. "What the hell?"

Sister Margaret raised her eyebrows. "You do have a key, though, right?"

"Yes, yes, of course." Tillie dug in her purse and pulled out her keys, fumbling a little with the lock, her mind furiously sorting through the names of anyone who might have wanted to put up a stitch-shield on her door.

Mattie might have benefitted from it when she was staying there, but she was so new to magery, it wouldn't have occurred to her. Nor would she know how to do it, being pretty much limited to spells that affected the here-and-now at this point.

Trevor might have thought of it – he was that kind of cautious person – but he wouldn't have the skill at spells.

As she pushed the door open, her mind landed on the man they were currently in search of. Giovani had the skills, the training, and the forethought. "But what was his motive?" she said aloud.

"Whose motive?" said Sister Catherine.

"It had to have been Giovani," Tillie said absently, as she moved toward the coffee table to pick up the note she'd left for him earlier, which was still laying on the hardwood floor. "But why? And when?"

"Guess we'll just have to ask him when we find him," said Sister Margaret. She roamed the condo, prowling the corners, picking up objects and setting them down, a little harder than Tillie would have liked. "I'm not sure what we're looking for here."

"Does anything look out of place to you, Tillie?" said Sister Catherine. "Anything that might tell us what he did when he woke up?"

Tillie looked around carefully, but nothing jumped out at her. She examined the paper she was holding, in case Giovani might have written a note back to her, but he hadn't. "Nothing I can see," she said. "I'll go look in the rest of the condo."

She poked her head into the bathroom, the spare room, and her own bedroom. Everything seemed normal there. In the kitchen, she saw a water glass sitting next to the sink, but there was nothing particularly suspicious about that.

Tillie returned to the living room to find everyone else seated and waiting for her. All heads turned as she entered, and she shrugged. "I guess we'll have to start fanning out. Maybe ask neighbors if they saw him?"

"Good plan," said Sister Catherine. "Do we have a picture we can show around?"

Tillie rummaged in her purse and pulled out her phone. "Trevor insisted we take some selfies after the battle on Friday and I think Giovani ended up in one of them."

Sister Margaret rolled her eyes. "Stitchers. Always have to document everything."

"Don't knock it," said Sister Catherine. "It's proving helpful now. And I can name half a dozen other times just off the top of my head when a picture I took helped me solve a problem later."

"Of course you can," said Sister Margaret with an affectionate smile.

"Here it is." Tillie found the photo and quickly cropped it to show only Giovani. She texted it to Sister Margaret, who was the only one present whose number she had. "Will you forward that to everyone here, please?"

"Yep." Sister Margaret fiddled with her own phone for a moment and then everyone's phones chimed their particular alert all at once. "I also forwarded it to my friend who lives in the building and asked her to ask around."

"All right, then, let's split up," said Tillie. She ushered more clergy than she'd ever thought would be in her home out into the hallway, assigning each a floor of the building. She took the second floor herself since they were her direct neighbors.

Then she began knocking on doors, starting with her friend Scott, who lived right next door.

***

"Okay, I think you've got the hang of the basics of seeing," said Sister Regina. "Now you have to learn

how to scry. Scrying is easier for spellers anyway –
you're actually just looking into the present."

Mattie frowned. "I can see the present anyway."

"No," said Sister Regina, speaking slowly as though
to a child. "Not the obvious present. You can look into
the present in another place or, in our case, you're
looking into the present in another mode. You'll be
looking at our subject's energy body instead of her
physical body."

Right. The hippy shit.

Mattie nodded and took a deep breath in. She'd been
practicing moving in and out of seer mode for about
half an hour and did feel like she was getting the hang
of it. It was the opposite of stitching, which required a
lot of focus.

Seer sight called for a complete lack of concentration,
almost like she sidled up to the future and pretended it
wasn't there, lulling it into a false sense of security until
she suddenly grabbed at it.

"Switch into seer mode again," Sister Regina
directed.

Mattie did so.

"Good," said Sister Regina. "Now filter out the
future and only see the present, but stay in seer mode."

"How?" asked Mattie.

"Just do it," Sister Regina snapped.

Mattie sighed. She was really starting to dislike
Sister Regina, and her high voice was grating on her
nerves.

But this had to be done, and Mattie was the one to
do it.

She forced herself to focus on the nun standing in
front of her, studiously ignoring the overlays of future-

Sister-Regina. She deliberately looked at the present incarnations of each person in the room, pushing her gaze quickly away from any future images that intruded.

Suddenly, the future disappeared, and all she could see was the present. "Got it!" she said, grinning triumphantly.

Sister Regina shoved the scrying stone into Mattie's face, holding it right in front of her eyes. "Now see the present in here!"

Mattie stared into the crystal and projected the image of the room into the clear globe. "I see it," she said.

"Now ask for the energy body!"

Mattie's mind stumbled. "Ask who?"

"I don't care who. Whoever you want. God, the universe, your imaginary friend. Just conjure it up," said Sister Regina.

"Like a spell?" Mattie felt on firmer ground here, and without waiting for an answer, she formed words in her mind, directing her magery to transform the figures in the scrying stone into beings of energy.

Immediately, all of the people in the stone changed from clothing-covered flesh people to people-shapes composed of glowing lines, connecting spinning brightly colored discs.

Most of them looked relatively uniform. The light-lines were golden and slowly moving, like rivers, their light flowing into the discs, which spun lazily. The colors of the discs were familiar from charts she'd seen of chakras in yoga studios and places like that.

Ida's lines and chakras were a little more faded than compared the others.

And Danielle and Nicole looked completely different.

Mattie gasped as she caught sight of the pair of them, sitting together on the love seat. As she studied them, she was vaguely aware of Ida's dimmer form coming over to her and putting a hand on her shoulder.

Ida must have been setting a spell to project her scrying onto the poster board, because a moment later, everyone else began swearing and exclaiming.

Danielle's light-lines – meridians, Mattie remembered they were called – were a deep, sullen red, sluggishly flowing into swollen, twitching chakras and then pulsing outward, as though the chakras were volcanos burping lava. Droplets of blood-red energy splashed out with each burst, dissipating into the air around her.

The chakras themselves were overall the same dark maroon but streaked with black that looked almost like a crust, deepening the impression of an erupting volcano.

Nicole looked even worse.

"Your prana is almost entirely black!" exclaimed Sister Regina. "How are you still alive?"

"I don't know," said Nicole, her voice trembling. "Can you fix it?"

"We're going to try," said Sister Regina grimly. "But I've never seen anything like this."

"This may be new territory," said Father Sean. "But we're all fully capable of dealing with it. We just have to have faith."

Easy for him to say. He was a priest.

Mattie stared at Nicole's energy, with its almost solid tarlike meridians and its barely moving chakras, and compared it to Father Sean's, which looked practically angelic.

"Faith is all very well," said Ida briskly. "But more to the point, we have skill and determination. Mattie, I think you can drop the scrying now. You must be exhausted."

"No, I can—"

Trevor put an arm around her. "You can't push yourself like that, Matts. Everyone needs a break. Just for a minute or two."

Reluctantly, Mattie shifted back out of seer mode and gasped as a massive headache hit her like a ton of bricks. She swayed and everything went black.

***

"Thanks, Brittany," said Tillie to the very last resident on the second floor of her building. "If you do see him, I'd appreciate a text."

"Yeah, no problem. Let me get your phone number," said Brittany.

"Of course." Tillie forced her face into a smile as yet another person she'd known for years asked for her phone number.

She'd had to introduce herself to all of them as, "Tillie's twin sister, Mattie. I moved into her condo when she passed away."

And then deal with all of the condolences and the, "Wow, you look just like your sister!" before finally getting on to the, "Have you seen this man? We're very concerned about his whereabouts."

And of course, even the ones who had Tillie's number in their phone didn't have Mattie's. And she couldn't very well give them her own number, because they already had that labeled as hers, and while it was pretty normal for someone to move into an inherited home, using a dead lady's phone would be super weird.

So she'd memorized Sister Margaret's number and given them that, instructing her to pretend to be Mattie if anyone texted about Giovani.

Heaven forbid anyone actually call – who knew what kind of voicemail message someone like Sister Margaret used. Plus the woman's voice was deeper than hers and had a noticeable accent.

For once, Tillie was glad Mattie had never come to visit until this whole rigmarole had started. If any of her neighbors had actually spent any time around Mattie, they'd see right through the ruse. Mattie would never be wearing a dress this short and low-cut, and, while she'd toned down the hair and make-up, Tillie hadn't been able to resist curling her bangs just a little and wearing a teensy bit of mascara and lip gloss.

She trudged back up the hall to her condo, only to find everyone else already waiting once again. "Sorry. I got sucked into a lot of conversation," she said, unlocking the door and letting them into the living room.

"We all struck out," said Sister Margaret. "Did you have any luck?"

"No," said Tillie. "No one saw him leave. Scott and Deanna both saw him arrive this morning. Deanna works nights and was probably just getting home. Not sure what Scott was doing."

"So, what next?" said Sister Margaret. "I say we fan out in triads. Speller, stitcher, seer together—"

"We only have one speller," Sister Catherine pointed out. "And we have three stitchers and two seers."

Tillie wandered over to her desk and picked up the notebook she'd been writing on that morning, staring numbly at the numbers she'd recorded. So much for their dozens of allies – now they were down to eleven mages. Everyone else was compromised.

Feeling very detached from reality, Tillie watched her arm reach out and pick up the pen, crossing out numbers and replacing them with big zeros. Then her arm tore the page from the notebook altogether and began methodically tearing it, first down the middle, then into quarters and smaller and smaller.

When a stack got too thick to tear, she split it up again, tearing as much as she could at a time and then moving on to the next piece.

She ripped the page, bit by bit, into confetti and then tossed it up into the air, watching it fall around her and wondering why she felt nothing. Was this despair?

Surely despair would be something, wouldn't it?

As suddenly as the nothingness had come upon her, Tillie found herself standing next to the door, off-balance and confused.

She put up a hand – voluntarily, she was pleased to note – and braced herself against the wall, then turned around to see the concerned faces of five nuns and a priest staring at her.

A hysterical giggle escaped her lips. It sounded like the start of a bad joke. "Five nuns and a priest walk into a bar," she murmured.

"What happened there?" asked Sister Catherine. "You looked like you were about to faint."

"Did anyone get a good look at her eyes?" Sister Margaret demanded.

"She was facing away from us all," said Father Bruce. "How do you feel, Tillie?"

Tillie glanced over at her desk. Her notebook still lay right where she left it, and no confetti littered the floor. "I – don't understand."

"Come and sit down, dear," said Sister Tim, taking Tillie's hand and guiding her to the couch. "You were closing the door and you started swaying for just a moment like you were going to fall down. Do you feel dizzy?"

"A little bit," Tillie admitted.

"What have you eaten today?" asked Sister Helen.

"Oh." Tillie suddenly realized that she had eaten literally nothing. She glanced at the clock on her wall. It was four o'clock in the afternoon, and she'd been up for over twelve hours and consumed only green tea and a few sips of blueberry cider. "I think I should probably get some protein in me."

"I'll get you something," said Sister Catherine, heading toward the kitchen.

"There are some protein shakes in the fridge," Tillie called after her.

Sister Catherine returned a few seconds later, turning the brown and white carton over and over as she walked to mix it up. She handed it to Tillie.

The cold carton felt good against Tillie's hand. She unscrewed the lid and took a big sip of the chocolate shake. She swallowed and felt the chill of it all the way down her throat. "Thank you."

"Okay," said Sister Margaret, "She's out. I still think fanning out and searching the neighborhood is our best bet. I'll take Sister Helen and Sister Tim."

Sister Catherine nodded at Father Bruce. "I guess that leaves us."

Tillie took another sip. She really should insist on coming along. They needed her.

Father Bruce placed a hand on Tillie's shoulder. "Get some rest, dear. We'll see you tomorrow morning, shall we?"

She downed the rest of her shake and stood up. "No, I can—" Tillie swayed again and her knees buckled. She landed hard on the edge of the sofa.

Tillie looked up at Father Bruce and gave him a wan smile. "What time?"

"Let's say nine o'clock," said Sister Catherine. "You can't help others if you don't take care of yourself."

Tillie nodded. "Will you text me if you find anything?"

"Of course," said Sister Catherine. "Now go to bed."

Tillie murmured her thanks as she folded down into a side-lying position on the couch. She grabbed a blanket and groped around for a cushion to put under her head. There was no way she was making it all the way to her bedroom.

5.

Mattie opened her eyes and saw a crowd of worried faces peering down at her. She sat up and whacked her forehead against something hard and wooden. "Oh, fuck," she muttered. "If I wasn't already going to have a bruise, I am now."

She realized that she was lying on the bottom bunk, still in Nicole and Danielle's cell. "How did I get over here?"

"You blacked out," said Trevor. "You almost fell off your chair, but I caught you and carried you over here."

"How gallant of you." Mattie propped herself up on her elbows, careful not to lift up high enough to hit her head again. "How long was I out?"

"Just a few minutes," said Nicole. "We pried up your eyelids and your eyes seemed normal. Any weird dreams or visions?"

Mattie carefully shook her aching head. "Not that I remember. I don't think I'm bespelled – just tired. But I'm feeling better now."

"None of us thought we were bespelled either," Danielle pointed out.

"I agree with Mattie," said Sister Regina. "No one else has fainted from the spell. Plus, I scanned her energy and it looks perfectly normal. She's clean."

"Great." Mattie swung her feet onto the floor. "Let's get back to work, then."

"Whoa!" said Trevor, gently pushing her chest back down onto the bed. "There's a lot of territory between not-under-a-spell and ready-to-do-draining-magework." He turned to Sister Regina. "You can take over on the seer duties for a while, right?"

She nodded. "I could, if we were going to continue."

"You don't think you can fix us," said Danielle. She sat down heavily and buried her face in her hands.

Sister Regina shook her head. "It's not that I don't think we can, full-stop. It's just that we can't right now. Look at us. We have one seer and one very inexperienced speller who can sort of fill in for a seer."

Mattie frowned. Sort of? She thought she'd been doing pretty well.

"I'm fine," she said, standing. She braced herself on the edge of the top bunk so no one would see how unsteady she felt.

Sister Regina ignored her. "That speller is now incapacitated. Of our other two spellers, one is extremely elderly and the other is disabled."

Mattie, Ida, and Father Sean all opened their mouths to protest, but Sister Regina plowed on. "I don't mean any offense – I'm just stating a fact. Ida, you look like you're on the verge of collapse, and Father Sean, I know you're good at your job, but you're not getting any younger either, and you do tend to tire quickly."

Mattie glanced at Ida and was shocked to see that the old woman was showing signs of wear. She was so used to thinking of her as invincible, but her normally straight back was slightly hunched and her eyes hooded. And she had been sort of wobbly earlier, hadn't she?

Sister Regina turned to Trevor. "And I understand that you're a very good stitcher for your experience level, but let's face it – how long have you been doing this?"

"About three weeks," he admitted.

"So, I'm sorry, but this is going to have to wait until we get some reinforcements in," said Sister Regina. "And I'm assuming, since we haven't heard from the other group, that they are still engaged with their own mission."

No one spoke for a few moments.

Mattie met Trevor's eyes and he gave her a small, tired smile that conveyed volumes of frustration with their current situation, bewilderment at the existence of the situation to begin with, and maybe even a question of whether they could still get out of the situation.

Trevor wasn't cut out for this kind of thing – he was a scholar, not a warrior. Not that Mattie thought of herself as a warrior either, but she'd get there.

Finally, Father Sean spoke. "So, what now?"

"We may as well all go home, I suppose," said Ida. Even her voice held some defeat. "Get some rest. Come back in the morning and try again. Everyone works better on a good night's sleep, I always say." She turned to Trevor. "If I could prevail upon you for a ride home, young man? I took the bus here and I'm not feeling up for it now."

"Of course," he said. He turned to Mattie. "You're getting a ride too, Matts. You're in no shape for biking."

"I'm—"

"You're not fine," said Trevor frowning at her. "You just fainted. I'm giving you a ride, and that's final."

Mattie sighed and nodded. Riding home with Trevor would be faster anyway.

Sister Regina headed off toward the convent's living quarters without any further goodbyes, and Mattie followed Trevor, Ida, and Father Sean up the stairs toward the parking lot.

None of them spoke until they were outside.

Mattie was faintly surprised that it was still light out – it felt like it should have been late, like midnight or later. She pulled her phone out of her jeans pocket. It was only a little after five o'clock.

Almost dinner time. Right on cue, her stomach rumbled.

Trevor grinned at her. "We'll drop Ida off and then go get some food," he said. "Take out. And bring it back to my place."

"Perfect," said Mattie. Maybe they could strategize while they ate.

Father Sean waved at them as he broke off from the group, jogging toward a beat-up brown Chevy sedan.

Mattie opened the back passenger door of Trevor's Subaru and slid in, letting Ida ride shotgun.

The trio was quiet as Trevor drove out of the lot and toward the neighborhood that all three of them lived in.

Finally, Ida broke the silence. "She's right, I suppose. I don't like her, but she's right."

"Who?" Mattie had been deep in thought, puzzling over the possible origins of the spell over her friends, and Ida's words startled her out of her reverie.

"Sister Regina," said Ida. "I am tired. Old and worn out. I think this will be my last war."

"Oh, Ida," Mattie began.

Ida waved away her objections. "I don't mean that in a morbid way. I just mean I'll be retiring after this. I retired from my job years ago. I should have retired from being a big bad mage warrior at the same time, I suppose." She sighed. "There are just so many causes, and I always have to butt my big nose in, I suppose."

Mattie smiled. "I'm sure a ton of lives have been saved because you butted your nose in."

"Big nose," corrected Ida with a laugh.

"And I know my life is better with you in it," Mattie continued.

"I'll drink to that," said Trevor. "Later, I mean, when I'm not driving."

"Well, thank you," said Ida. "I didn't intend to get mixed up in this one, really. And then I thought I would take more of an advisory role after the battle, but then this whole weird spell thing came up, and I just can't seem to step aside, I suppose."

"You were made for action," said Mattie. "But if you need to rest, maybe you should sit tomorrow out. We can manage without you."

"No, no," said Ida. "I'm in it now! We'll solve this one last problem – and maybe I'll do it from a seated position – and then I'm out. You all can take down the rest of the organization without me, I suppose." She paused. "Or maybe with me managing, but not fighting. Really, I have to see what happens. And the best place to see it is from the inside, I always say."

Mattie laughed. "You really are invincible, Ida."

Ida shook her head, her face uncharacteristically sober. "I'm not. Like I said, Sister Regina was right. And she'll get to this point too, and she'll remember what she said to me and she'll feel bad about it. But that doesn't make her any less right. I'm just about done."

They sank into another uncomfortable silence until they reached Ida's house.

Mattie waited in the car as Trevor escorted the old woman to her front door, noting as she watched that the past few days had indeed taken a toll on Ida's strength. She leaned against Trevor, moving more slowly than usual, her typically straight back slightly hunched.

Exiting the back seat and moving up to the front, Mattie resolved to keep an eye on her friend the next day, if she insisted on coming along. She wasn't one to tell another adult what they could and couldn't do, but she also didn't want Ida to have a heart attack or something.

Trevor came back to the car and they drove off in search of victuals.

"We need to do our best to make sure Ida takes it easy tomorrow," said Trevor, echoing Mattie's thoughts. "After all, tomorrow will be about strategy, maybe some group magic, if we can figure out something to do about this spell."

"Right," Mattie agreed. "No reason there should be any fighting or action. And it sounded to me like it'll be mostly stitching and seer-work, right?"

"Ida shouldn't need to be involved at all."

Mattie chewed on her bottom lip. "Do you think we could convince her to stay at home and rest?"

Trevor shook his head. "I've known Ida Garaveldi for a few years now. Granted, for most of that time, I had no idea she was a mage or even that mages existed. But in the time I've lived next door to her, I've seen her face down everyone from overly excitable door-to-door missionaries to an actual mafia stooge who tried to shake her down for protection money."

Mattie laughed. "Seriously? I'm going to need that story at some point."

Grinning, Trevor shook his head. "I have a feeling that I don't know the whole story, since it happened before. I'm guessing she left some stuff out when I asked her about it later."

He pulled into the parking lot of an Italian deli, parking near the door. He turned off the car and turned to face Mattie, squaring his shoulders as though psyching himself up for something unpleasant.

Mattie, about to open the car door, paused. "Is something wrong?"

Trevor spoke quickly. "You have to take it easy too, Matts. Please. I can see what you're doing, and I've seen you do it before, and it never ends well."

Mattie stared at him, her brow furrowed. "What are you talking about?"

He sighed and rubbed his temples. "Remember after your parents died? And you threw yourself into school? You had to get into all the best programs, had to reach for the stars, had to make something of yourself."

"What's wrong with being ambitious?" Mattie lifted her chin and crossed her arms.

"Nothing." Trevor's face was compassionate, his voice gentle.

Somehow that made Mattie feel terrible, like she was doing something wrong. Which she wasn't. She narrowed her eyes. Where did he get off, guilt-tripping her like this? "Then what's the problem here?"

"You burnt yourself out," said Trevor. "You drove yourself too hard and you closed yourself off to everyone else and—"

"And I realized it and took a step back," said Mattie. "This is different. I was eighteen. I think I've grown a little since then."

"Have you?" Trevor raised an eyebrow. He ran a hand over his close-cropped black hair. "Look, I'm not trying to criticize, Matts, I'm worried about you."

Mattie turned her back on him, opening her car door and getting out. "Let's just get some food," she said.

***

Tillie awoke very suddenly and sat up quickly, clutching the blanket to her chest, eyes darting around the semi-darkness of her living room, struggling to identify the sound that had awoken her. "Must have been a dream," she said aloud after a few moments.

She dropped the blanket and rose to her feet, stretching tall and then adjusting her dress. "I can't believe I fell asleep in this." One of her breasts had popped out of its low neckline, and she carefully tucked it back in.

BANG BANG BANG! She whirled toward the sound, her eyes automatically switching into seer mode as she scanned the wall beside the linen closet. "Oh, you have got to be fucking kidding me! Giovani?"

Tillie snapped out of seer mode and strode to the desk, pulling open a drawer and snatching out a talisman in one smooth motion. She carefully fitted the symbol on the talisman into the carved-out indentation on the closet door, activating the secret entrance to her ritual room.

As the door slid open, Giovani fell through it, collapsing into a rumpled puddle of a man at her feet. He rolled over and looked up at her. "Tillie?"

Tillie took a step backward so he wasn't looking up her skirt. "We have been looking everywhere for you!" she scolded. "Have you seriously been in there the whole time?"

"I don't know," he said. "What whole time?"

Tillie threw up her hands. "All day! All evening!" She glanced at the clock on the wall. "It's the middle of the night now. What happened? How did you even get in there? You can't stitch in there, and you're not supposed to be able to close the door from the inside."

"I don't know," he said again. His stomach rumbled. "Did you say it's the middle of the night?"

"When did you last eat?" Tillie demanded.

"When did you give me those cookies?"

"Dammit! You haven't eaten in twenty hours? You're as bad as I am."

He smiled weakly up at her. "That sounds about right."

Tillie bent down and reached out a hand. "Get up. Come on. We have to get you to the convent. They'll feed you there."

"The convent?" he frowned. "Why?"

"I'll tell you on the way. Come on." She wiggled her fingers at him and he grasped her hand, pulling himself up.

His hand was freezing.

"You look like you slept in your clothes," he observed.

"So do you," she said. "I have some of Trevor's clothes and you're shaped about the same. Shorter, but I think they'll fit you okay. Let's get changed before we go." She led the way toward the bedrooms and pointed into the guest room. "Bottom drawer of the dresser in there."

Tillie continued into her own room and grabbed a pair of jeans, a tank top, and a cardigan, changing quickly. She went into the bathroom and glanced in the mirror. Her hair was standing up on one side and her mascara was smeared, raccoon-like around her eyes.

Grinning at herself, she ran her hands back and forth over her head, creating a huge frizz of hair. She spent a couple of minutes rearranging it in sillier and sillier configurations before finally picking up her brush and smoothing it out into waves.

She shook her head at herself. There wasn't time for this kind of ridiculousness.

Tillie quickly wiped off her eye make-up and refreshed it.

When she returned to the living room, Giovani was already there waiting.

Stopping short, Tillie stared. He was wearing a grey polo shirt and a pair of black slacks. "You look like when you see an actor out of character," Tillie told him. "I've never seen you wearing anything other than a beige suit."

"I can't remember the last time I wore anything other than that," said Giovani. "It's been my schtick ever since I became an Auditor agent."

Tillie grabbed her purse from the coffee table where she'd dropped it earlier. "The beige suits look good on you, but maybe it's time to lose that identity," she suggested as she led the way out the door.

"In favor of this?" Giovani sounded unsure.

"No." Tillie laughed. "I love Trevor, but he dresses like a nerd." She started down the stairs, looking back at him over her shoulder as she talked. "How did you dress before the organization?"

Giovani was silent for a moment. "I don't know. Just normal."

Tillie paused, turning sideways and leaning against the banister to regard Giovani. She studied his lean body, lingering on his arms, which were usually covered and were pleasantly muscled in a not-overbearing way.

She shut down that line of thought, moving back toward the original point. "I don't really know what 'normal' is – everyone has their own idea – but I think you should consider a more casual style."

"I like wearing the same thing every day," objected Giovani, walking past her to continue down the stairs. "It's easy."

Tillie followed him, He did look good in those jeans. "You can still have a simple wardrobe," she objected.

"But your beige suits are so boring. And you're not boring."

"I like being underestimated." He rounded the corner, pushing through the glass door to the atrium.

Tillie glanced over at her mailbox and saw the corner of an envelope poking through the slats on the front. How long had it been since her mail had been emptied? "Hold on a sec," she said, pulling her keys out. She opened the mailbox and letters burst out, spilling onto the counter underneath. "Dammit."

Giovani helped her gather all the mail and she stuffed it into her purse to peruse later.

"Thanks," she said. "Let's go. Do you have your car nearby?"

"Yeah." Giovani led her down a side alleyway to the black SUV he'd stolen from the Auditor garage.

"I'm surprised this is still here," Tillie commented. "I don't think you're supposed to park here."

Giovani shrugged. "I always park in alleys. People just assume if they see a car in an alley, that someone is just running in to grab something. You just can't leave it for more than a day or two. Then it gets towed. But I'm rarely around for more than that."

Tillie slid onto the smooth leather upholstery of the passenger seat. "This is nice. At least they set you all up with decent cars."

"Oh, no, this is definitely not an agent car," said Giovani, clicking on his seatbelt. "They keep a couple nicer vehicles around for the court to use. Agents get unassuming cars. They say it's so we'll blend in, but I'm sure they're just cheap."

"Well, anyway, you made a good choice," said Tillie.

"Why are we going to the convent again?" asked Giovani as he pulled out onto the street.

Tillie opened her mouth to tell him and found that her voice wasn't working. She mouthed the words and nothing came out.

She coughed.

"You okay?" Eyes still on the road, Giovani reached his arm into the backseat and pulled out an unopened bottle of water. "Here. It's been sitting in the car, so it's not cold. Sorry."

"Thanks," Tillie croaked. She opened the bottle and took a long sip. She grimaced. It was unpleasantly warm. "Sorry. Not sure what happened there."

Her voice had resumed normalcy, but she couldn't remember what they had been talking about. She shrugged inwardly. Couldn't have been important. "You know how to get there, right?"

Giovani stopped at a red light and turned to face her. "Yes, but you still haven't told me why we need to get there. It sounded like it was urgent. Did something happen?"

Oh, yeah, that's what they had been talking about. The light changed to green and she nodded toward it. "Green light."

"Right." Giovani turned his attention back to the road.

Tillie opened her mouth again to tell him about the weird spell affecting the rebel agents, but once more, the words simply would not emerge.

She cleared her throat. That was weird – she could make sounds now. She took another sip of water.

What was she even going to say before? She couldn't remember. Well, the convent wasn't far.

Wait a second. Now she couldn't remember why they were going to the convent. Maybe Mattie had texted her?

Tillie pulled her phone out of her purse and checked her texts from Mattie. The last one was about moving a meeting up. "What meeting?" Tillie asked aloud.

"What?" Giovani glanced over at her again and then yelped. "What the hell is wrong with your eyes?"

Tillie blinked. "What? What do you mean?" She pulled down the visor to check in the mirror.

"Look at me," said Giovani. The car was stopped at another light, and Tillie turned toward him so he could look.

Giovani relaxed. "Okay, it must have just been a shadow or something. I could have sworn your eyes were pure black for a second. It was really creepy."

Tillie frowned. "That sounds familiar somehow."

He shrugged. "Maybe it's from a movie or something."

The light changed again, and he continued driving toward the convent.

Tillie uncovered the mirror, checking her eyes. They looked completely normal.

"So, why are we going to the convent again?" Giovani asked one more time.

"I honestly cannot remember," said Tillie. "Maybe we don't need to go there after all. Maybe I had a dream that we did and it was still fresh in my mind when I woke up. I don't know."

"Okay, well, I'm starving. Maybe we could stop for food, at least," Giovani suggested.

"Oh, yes, that sounds great," Tillie agreed. "There's actually an amazing twenty-four-hour diner just a couple blocks away."

He raised an eyebrow, looking at her sideways. "You don't strike me as a diner person."

Tillie shrugged. "Where else do you think we'd be able to go at this time of the night? Pull in here." She pointed to a small parking lot.

Giovani obliged, parking the car in the single empty spot. He turned off the car and opened his door. "Sure, but you've been there often enough to call it 'amazing?'"

She hopped out of the car and walked around to his side to poke him in the chest playfully. "Look. Ninety percent of the time, I want organic veggies and farm-to-table cuisine that costs an arm and a leg. But there's always that other ten percent, when a fucking slinger hits the spot."

She spun on her heel and began leading him down the street.

Giovani jogged to catch up. "Oh, my God, I forgot about slingers. Tillie, I haven't had a slinger since I was ripped from the bosom of St. Louis's culinary masters ten years ago." He grabbed her hand and began dragging her down the street.

Tillie laughed as she pulled her hand from his and skipped ahead. "Last one there picks up the check."

Giovani suddenly appeared a block ahead of her. "Amateur!" he taunted.

She laughed again and pulled open the door to the diner. "It helps to know where the place is! And stitching is cheating!"

"Joke's on you," said Giovani, trotting back toward her. "I don't have any money."

She stuck out her tongue at him as he walked through the door she held open. The place smelled of bacon, burnt grease, and ever so slightly of cigarettes, still hanging on from the days when you could smoke in restaurants.

"Two of you?" said the tired-looking bottle-blonde behind the counter. "Just sit anywhere. And if you could tell me now how drunk you are and which drugs you're on, that would save us all a lot of trouble."

"Not at all and none," said Tillie. "We've just had a long day." She led Giovani to a booth up against the window.

"You and me both, honey," said the woman. She brought them a couple of laminated menus, setting them down and pulling out a notepad and pen. The nametag pinned to her yellow dress said Ruth. "Coffee?"

"None for me," said Tillie. "Green tea if you've got it."

"I'll take some coffee," said Giovani. "With sugar, please. And I don't need a menu. I'll have a slinger, over-easy, side of gravy."

"Toast?"

"Sourdough, if you've got it."

Ruth nodded, finished writing, and looked at Tillie expectantly, her pen hovering.

"Same, sans gravy," said Tillie. "Extra bacon on the side."

"Oh, yes, extra bacon for me too," said Giovani. "And if it's not too much trouble, is there something ready right now I could munch on while that's cooking?"

"Cottage cheese or a fruit cup?"

"Fruit cup," he said. "Thank you."

Ruth gathered up the menus and plodded off without another word.

"So, now that food is in sight, tell me what happened to you today and how you got into my ritual room." Tillie leaned back in the booth, eyes fixed on Giovani's face.

"Like I said, I don't know." Giovani ran a hand over his stubbled chin. "I guess I fell asleep on your couch this morning. Sorry about that, by the way."

Tillie waved a hand in dismissal. "You're welcome anytime." She frowned. "Where are you living right now, anyway?"

"Aaron and I got an apartment a couple blocks away from Auntie Ida's house," he said. "It doesn't feel like a home yet. Your place feels personal. I guess that's why I was able to sleep so easily."

Ruth returned to the table with a laden tray, setting down a mug of coffee and a cup of sliced melons and pineapple in front of Giovani and a pot of hot water and a mug with a teabag in it in front of Tillie.

She set a small plate between them that held colorful packets of various sweeteners. "The rest will be out in a few minutes," she said. "Do y'all need any ketchup or hot sauce?"

"Hot sauce, please," said Tillie.

Ruth nodded and walked back to her post behind the counter, settling herself on a stool and opening up a well-worn novel.

"Yeah, but aren't you used to traveling all the time?" said Tillie, pouring water over her teabag.

"I'm *tired* of traveling all the time," Giovani corrected. He sipped his coffee, closing his eyes in bliss.

So, he was one of those people who thought coffee was some sort of magical ambrosia that tasted like paradise and cured all ills. Tillie repressed a smirk. How unexpectedly mundane of him.

"Fair enough," she said. "Okay, so you fell asleep. I know that. You were still asleep when I left. How long did you sleep?"

Giovani scooped a spoonful of fruit into his mouth and chewed slowly. He seemed to be trying to remember. "I'm not sure," he said finally. "I had these dreams, but I'm not sure all of them really were dreams...."

A chill overtook Tillie and she shivered violently.

Giovani lifted an eyebrow. "Are you cold?"

She shook her head. "Someone must have walked over my grave, I guess," she deflected. "Tell me about the dreams." She frowned. "I feel like I've heard something about dreams lately. Were they about the Pontiff?"

He leaned forward. "How did you know?"

"I don't know." Tillie shook her head again, feeling slightly dizzy.

Giovani's brow furrowed and he leaned forward, peering into Tillie's eyes. "Are you sure you're okay?"

"I don't know," said Tillie again. "Something feels wrong, but I can't put a finger on it. You know, I haven't eaten much today – yesterday – either. It's probably just that."

"Sure." Giovani nodded. "That makes sense. The first one was definitely a dream. I was back in training with the organization." His voice trembled slightly, and Tillie's heart ached for him. "My class was sparring, just practicing our hand-to-hand combat, and my instructor suddenly yelled at us to stop what we were doing and line up against the wall."

A bell dinged from the kitchen, and Tillie and Giovani both jumped in startlement. Their eyes met and they shared an uneasy laugh.

Ruth got up from her stool and disappeared through the swinging door.

"We lined up, and the Pontiff walked in. He looked younger, like he probably would have when I was in training."

"Was this something that actually happened?" Tillie asked. She pulled the bag from her tea, wrapping the string around it, careful not to burn her fingers as she squeezed all the essence from the hot teabag.

Giovani shook his head. "Definitely not. In fact, I never even saw the Pontiff until about three years ago."

He paused as Ruth bustled out of the kitchen, her hands and arms laden with plates.

She hurried to their table and began distributing dishes. "Okay, I've got two slingers, both over-easy. Sourdough toast. Here's a side of gravy for you . . . and hot sauce for you . . . and there's two orders of extra bacon, but the cook put it all on one plate; I hope that's okay."

Having unburdened herself of everything, she took a step back and surveyed the table, hands on her hips. "That's it, right?"

Tillie looked it over as well. "This looks fantastic. Thank you."

"You need anything else?" Ruth eyed Giovani as she picked up the empty cup that had held his fruit. "Ketchup? OJ? More coffee?"

"I'm good," said Giovani with a smile.

"I'll be right over there," said Ruth. She hurried back to her book without further ado.

In unspoken accord, Tillie and Giovani paused their conversation to give proper attention to their plates.

Tillie unwrapped her cutlery from their tightly wound napkin. She placed the napkin on her lap and then picked up the fork, stabbing her eggs to release the runny yolks into the chili that covered them. Next, she grabbed her half of the extra bacon and arranged it over the top. Then she sprinkled hot sauce over the entire mess, and finally, picked up her toast and used her fork to cut into the hashbrowns and scoop a bite of every glorious layer of slinger onto it.

She bit into the toast and closed her eyes blissfully. Tell anyone who wasn't from St. Louis that they should start smothering their breakfast in chili, and they'll look at you like you're insane. But anyone who's ever had a slinger knows . . . it's the ultimate diner comfort food.

Tillie glanced over at Giovani, who was having his own moment of nirvana. She wrinkled her nose at the gravy he had poured over his.

Giovani paused, midbite, as he noticed her regard. "What?"

She shook her head, a small smile playing about her lips. "Nothing. Enjoy your food."

He narrowed his eyes. "I am enjoying it."

"Good!" Tillie's smile widened. "So what's the problem?"

"I can see you over there, judging me. You're a purist, aren't you?"

"I just don't see the point of the gravy. Slingers are perfect as they are. Why add to something that's already perfect?"

He studied her. "Have you ever tried it with gravy?"

"Well, no," she admitted.

Giovani grabbed her toast out of her hand and loaded it up from his plate. "Anyway, you add hot sauce. How is that different?"

"Hot sauce is a condiment," she said. "It's not a whole new ingredient."

He handed her toast back to her and leaned on his elbows against the table. "Just try it."

Tillie eyed the gravy with resignation. "Fine." She took a bite and chewed. Uh oh. It was amazing. There was a depth of flavor there that just—"Dammit," she said, her mouth still full. She swallowed. "You're right."

He grinned. "Of course I am. Never doubt me again."

She shook her head. "No, I'm still going to take that on a case-by-case basis."

"Fair enough." Giovani took another bite of food. "Where was I when I was so sublimely interrupted?"

"Your dream." Tillie grabbed the cup of gravy and scraped the meager remains onto her own plate. "You lined up against the wall and the Pontiff walked in."

"Yeah. So, he comes in and he's looking us over like they do in movies, you know, where new recruits are in boot camp and some superior officer comes in to check out the fresh blood and then gives them a pep talk."

"Sure."

"I can't really remember what he said to us. I just remember he was speaking and then his hands started glowing, and I knew without a doubt that he had put some kind of spell on us. And then the glow went away." Giovani drained the last of his coffee and waved to Ruth, saluting her with his mug when she glanced over.

Ruth ambled over with a metal carafe of coffee and refilled his mug. "Can I get some of this out of your way for you?" Without waiting for an answer, she began gathering up the empty side plates and then sauntered away.

Giovani continued his story. "And then I thought I woke up, but I must have still been dreaming, because I wasn't at your condo. I was in a motel room."

Tillie raised an eyebrow. "A familiar motel room?"

"Aren't they all?" Giovani shrugged. "I've been in a lot of motel rooms in the past ten years, and while sometimes you get one that's kind of different, kitschy or retro, those usually cost more. The organization is only going to spring for the novelty motels if there's nothing else around. This was just a standard room. Two beds, a table and a chair, a dresser with an old microwave on it. Anyway, so I was in the motel room, waking up. But I wasn't sure at first what woke me up, so I pretended I was still asleep and just looked around carefully. The other bed was in my line of sight and I could see that it was empty and still made up, like no one had slept there."

He paused as though waiting for a reaction.

"Were you expecting someone to be there?" asked Tillie.

Giovani nodded. "My partner should have been in the other bed. Agent Powell."

Tillie choked on her tea. Somehow, it had never occurred to her that Giovani would have been working with a partner. Of course he did, though – they all did. "What happened to Agent Powell?"

"In the dream?" he asked. "Or in real life?"

"Both, I guess."

He shrugged. "In real life, I ditched him. I decided I was leaving the organization. I was in St. Louis, my hometown, and had been thinking about leaving for a while, and it just seemed like kismet that I was here. And then everything else that happened that morning seemed like a sign. Including what Agent Powell said to me."

"You never did tell me what happened," said Tillie.

Giovani was silent and still for a moment.

"You don't have to tell me," said Tillie. "Or you can tell me another time."

He shook himself free of his reverie. "No, it's fine. All good. In a nutshell, I ran into the Agents who were assigned your case, and Agent Miller said something about you."

"What was it?" Tillie leaned forward, curious what had made Giovani choose to save her, of all people.

"She said she thought you were going to be a challenge. That you'd try to run."

Tillie frowned. "How did she know that?"

"I don't know. It was an odd thing for a stitcher to say," said Giovani. "In retrospect, I almost wonder if she was sounding me out. Seeing what I thought about someone who would run. Maybe she just said that to all the agents she met for the first time, to see if they'd be interested in joining her rebellion."

"Right," said Tillie.

"But it got me thinking. If you ran, maybe you could escape. If I helped you. I'd been secretly practicing my spelling again, and I think it made me impulsive. I broke into Agent Miller's room and looked at her file on you, put your address and description into my phone. But I still wasn't sure. Agent Powell was a new partner – I didn't know him very well yet. My old partner had been killed in action, another thing that I think was making me doubt the lifestyle, if you know what I mean.

"I ran into Powell on my way back to my room, and without really thinking about it, I asked him if he'd ever thought about leaving. He gave me the oddest look, almost triumphant, as though he'd caught me at something. And he said, 'Hardly ever.'"

Tillie's eyebrows rose. "Hardly ever? What does that mean?"

Giovani shook his head. "I don't really know. But in the moment, I took it as a sign. I don't even really know why. I think I was going to take every little thing as a sign. That's the thing about signs – it's easy to find them if you're looking. But if a straight-laced company-man type like Powell sometimes thought about leaving, then dammit, so could I.

"I went back to my room, packed my bag, and stole a car from the garage. Then I went to a drug store and stole a burner phone and some cash, ditched my old phone as soon as I transferred all the info I'd need, and came to find you. You know the rest. I haven't seen

Powell since. He wasn't in St. Louis anymore when we got back here, so he must have gotten a new assignment."

"Huh." Tillie wiped down her plate with the corner of her toast, chasing down every little bit of chili, gravy, and egg yolk. She popped it into her mouth and chewed slowly, savoring the last bite as she considered his story. "So, he's just out there, then. Wondering what happened to you."

"He probably assumes I was killed," said Giovani.

"Even though you weren't on assignment?" Tillie frowned. "Who would have killed you?"

"Probably another agent. Sparring can get out of hand and dueling isn't uncommon either," said Giovani. "Courtiers sometimes get pissy or bored and kill an agent too, and nobody does anything about it. That's not as common."

Tillie frowned. "But the court wasn't here yet."

"No, but there are always a few courtiers who don't travel with the rest. Either because they have some kind of bureaucratic job to do or because they just feel like taking a vacation and staying in some random HQ."

"Wait a second." Tillie leaned forward, wrapping her hands around her tea mug. "I was under the impression that there were just a few stragglers out there. How many courtiers would you say are still at large because they weren't in St. Louis when we ambushed the court?"

He shrugged. "Maybe fifty? A hundred? The real threat is the agents, if they start getting their shit together and decide we're a threat. There are a lot more of them."

"How many?"

"In the United States alone, probably a couple thousand."

"And in the world?"

"I have no idea."

"Well, fuck." Tillie sipped her green tea. She was too tired to deal with this new perspective. "Anyway. Back to your dream. The bed was empty."

"Yeah. So I closed my eyes and flipped over, pretending to be just turning over my sleep, in case someone hostile was in the room."

"Was that a common occurrence when you were on the road?"

"No, but I've always been paranoid. I turned on my seer sight and opened my eyes a little bit, just enough to see if there was anyone around and if anything was going to happen. Nothing seemed out of place, and the future didn't show anyone or anything, so I opened my eyes all the way and sat up. The room was empty and nothing was supposed to happen."

"I take it something did happen, though?" Tillie shivered again. The idea that seer sight might not be one hundred percent effective filled her with unease. She told herself it was just a dream, and not even her own dream.

But was it just a dream? There was something creepy going on here, wasn't there? Something teased the edges of her mind, but she just couldn't remember....

Giovani looked down at his plate, pushing the remnants of his breakfast around. He dropped his fork and took a big gulp of coffee before continuing, with the air of someone fortifying themselves with whisky. "Someone attacked me."

"Who?"

"I don't know! I couldn't see them."

"They were using an invisibility spell?" Tillie frowned. "Had you turned off your seer sight?"

"No." He took another swig of coffee. "Do they sell booze here?"

She shook her head. "Not at this time of the night. Missouri's laws are pretty strict. So, you should have been able to see through any kind of sight shield or invisibility spell."

"Exactly," said Giovani. "Honestly, it was terrifying. Probably the worst dream I've ever had."

"So, what happened next?"

"I fought back. With everything I had. I kept my seer sight on and I put up shield spells. I started stitching myself into random positions in the room to keep out of their reach. If they were going to cheat, so was I, dammit." His hands were clenched so tightly around his coffee mug that they were turning white.

Tillie reached across the table and gently tugged at his fingers. "You're going to break that thing, and then Ruth will kill us and our friends will be that much more short-handed."

Something about the rebel agents being incapacitated…. Tillie shut her eyes and tried to remember. The memory escaped again, and she sighed and opened her eyes.

Giovani leaned forward suddenly, peering into her face.

"What?" she asked, started.

"I don't know." Giovani grabbed her chin across the table, holding her face still and studying her eyes. "Your eyes. They . . . flickered."

"What?" Tillie stared at him, trying not to blink. "Like, into seer mode? Are they doing it now?"

There was something about eyes too, wasn't there? Why couldn't she remember?

Giovani watched her for another few seconds and then released her face, leaning back in the booth again. "No. I must have imagined it. It wasn't like seer mode. They were black, like I thought I saw earlier. But I'm just tired. Sorry."

Tillie shook her head. "Don't be sorry. You've been through a lot."

"Right. Yeah."

"So, what happened next?" she asked. "In the dream?"

"He started hissing and calling me an abomination, just what you'd expect if he was an Auditor agent. Only I don't know how an agent would have made his spell impervious to seer magery. I mean, I think you could do it if you were morphing maybe, like combining a spell and a stitch to make it seem like he wasn't there, but an agent wouldn't do that."

"A courtier could," Tillie pointed out. "And they don't seem to have an issue with the hypocrisy of it."

"The voice sounded familiar," said Giovani. "It was cold and hard and filled with hate."

"Like the Pontiff," said Tillie.

Giovani froze. "Exactly like the Pontiff," he said slowly. "It was the Pontiff's voice. I don't know how I didn't make that connection, especially since I had just had that other dream."

"I'm so glad that guy is dead," said Tillie. "The bastard majorly gave me the creeps. What happened next?"

"We fought. For what seemed like hours. And then I woke up in the dark. I found my phone in my pocket, turned on the flashlight, realized I was in your ritual room, and started pounding on the door. You know the rest."

"Wait, that's it?" Tillie sat back in the booth, thoroughly confused. "You really have no idea how you got in there?"

"No. Like I said." Giovani stretched his arms upward. "To be honest, I feel like I really have been fighting for hours. My body aches and my mage energy feels depleted. At first, I thought it was just hunger, but I'm not hungry anymore and I still feel it."

Tillie glanced at his arms as he lowered them. She frowned and held out her hand. "Let me see that."

"What?"

"Your arms. What did you do to them?"

His brow furrowed, but he obligingly held out his arms.

Tillie leaned forward to examine them. "Did you have these bruises before? I don't remember seeing them earlier when we left the condo." Both of his arms were mottled with patches of discoloration and they were getting darker by the minute. Based on Tillie's own experience with hand-to-hand combat, she could see that the patterns fit.

Giovani looked closely too, prodded one of the bruises. "Ow!" His eyes met hers. "I can't think of any other way I could have gotten these. And the timing fits – I've always bruised quickly, so they would be forming now-ish if I had been fighting right before I woke up."

He pulled up his shirt a little, twisting to study his torso.

Even across the table, Tillie could see a few more bruises dappling his distractingly fit abs. "So, what does this mean?" she asked.

"I don't know." Giovani dropped his shirt back into place and rubbed his temples. "All I know is that this is fucking weird. And that I need some actual sleep, not sleep in which I'm fighting the ghost of the Pontiff."

"Right. Good idea." Tillie waved to Ruth. "We'll take the check, please."

6.

Mattie's phone alarm went off at 8:30 and she bounced up. She'd slept soundly and she felt rested, refreshed, and ready to face the day. She hummed as she reached into her dresser drawers and grabbed whatever was on top – jeans and one of her favorite well-worn t-shirts, which read *Don't Talk to Me – I'm Reading*.

As she moved out of her bedroom, she sobered slightly, regarding her housemates' empty bedrooms. Today they would fix the spell, and Nicole and Danielle would be back to kicking ass with the rest of them soon.

She refused to acknowledge any other possible outcome.

Mattie shivered slightly as she remembered the vast difference between the bespelled women's energy bodies and the normal ones of the others.

"Hippy shit or no, that was terrifying," she murmured to her reflection in the mirror as she ran a quick brush through her long red hair. It was a little flat on one side, where she'd slept on it without bothering to dry it first after her shower the night before. The other side poofed out like an untamable lion's mane.

Oh, well, it's not like she was going to a ball or something.

She grabbed a rubber band and pulled it back into a ponytail. Good enough.

Then she headed to the kitchen.

Mattie filled the kettle for her morning tea and gathered up everything she'd need for a simple breakfast of eggs and toast. The kettle sang and she plunked an English breakfast teabag in a ceramic mug and poured the boiling water over it.

As Mattie bustled about her kitchen, she felt almost normal. Almost as though she was back in her cozy studio apartment in Portland, getting ready to go teach English to a bunch of ungrateful teenagers.

She looked around. This little house was just as cozy, and while she wasn't used to roommates, Nicole and Danielle were good ones. When they weren't under a bizarre spell that turned them against her.

The feeling of normalcy faded and Mattie sighed as she flipped over the eggs in the frying pan. Her toast popped up and she turned off the stove, leaving the eggs to cook a little more from the residual heat and opening a drawer for a butter knife.

A knock sounded on the door. Mattie dropped the knife, her breath catching in her throat as she backed up a pace. Then she laughed at herself. If it was an enemy mage, they probably wouldn't bother knocking.

Mattie relaxed her face, just as she'd learned the night before, and switched into seer sight. She hadn't quite gotten her sister's knack for looking through walls, but she watched herself open the door and let Trevor into the house.

Grinning, Mattie switched her eyes back to normal and skipped over to the door, opening it up and stepping back with a flourish to admit her friend.

There had been a little bit of awkwardness the night before, but Mattie knew his heart was in the right place.

He just didn't understand that she needed to make sure everyone was safe, especially Tillie. She'd abandoned her sister before, but that was the old Mattie. The new Mattie would take care of Tillie.

And then everything could go back to normal. As soon as the Auditors were destroyed.

"Well!" he said, moving past her. "Aren't we chipper this morning?"

She raised her eyebrows and gave him an impish smile. "Are we?"

"You are," said Trevor. "I didn't sleep so well."

"No weird dreams?" she said, her smile fading as she eyed him warily.

Trevor shook his head. He led her into the kitchen and filled up her kettle again. "No dreams that I remember. I'm not turning Auditor or anything. Just restless. My brain going a million miles a minute."

"Sure," said Mattie. "There's coffee if you want. Nicole and Danielle are both coffee fiends."

"No, I already had some, and I'm going to be too jittery if I have more." Trevor drummed his fingers as he waited for the kettle, apparently already pretty on edge.

"Have you eaten?" Mattie asked.

"Yeah, go ahead," he said.

Relieved that she wasn't going to have to wait any longer, Mattie picked up her plate and settled down at the table in the small breakfast nook just off the kitchen.

"I was going to bike in today," she said. "But since you're here, you can give me a ride."

"That's why I'm here," said Trevor. "Your bike is still at the convent, remember? And I figured we could rehash everything, maybe put our heads together on whether we think what we did last night actually worked." He paused. "We didn't get a lot of productive talking done last night."

Mattie sighed. "We're okay. Let's rehash."

Trevor smiled. "Good."

Rehashing wasn't really Mattie's strong suit, but Trevor was a stitcher. Funny how quickly she'd fallen into the mage habit of categorizing everyone based on how their temperament related to their talents.

"I'm surprised you're here instead of picking up Tillie," she remarked.

"I texted her," said Trevor. "You're on my way to her place anyway. She said she had a long night herself."

"And Ida?" said Mattie.

Trevor shrugged. "I knocked on her door, but she didn't answer, so I'm hoping she decided to take the day off after all and get some rest."

"Fair enough," said Mattie. "Did the others ever find Giovani? I guess not, since we never heard from anyone about it."

Trevor shrugged, sitting down across from her and sipping his tea. "That would be my guess too."

"At least he hasn't attacked any of us," said Mattie, trying to look on the bright side. "Personally, I doubt I'd be able to fight him off – he's the strongest morpher we have."

Trevor nodded. "I'd definitely be fucked."

"So, do you have any ideas about what we can do to help the others?" said Mattie, sopping up some errant egg yolk with her toast.

"I wouldn't even know where to start," said Trevor. He sighed and ran a hand over his very short black hair. "I just don't know enough about anything to know. Sister Regina said it best. We've been throwing ourselves into this, but we're so new at it."

Mattie nodded. "Same boat here. And it doesn't help that none of the people who've been doing this shit for years seem to have a damn clue about it either."

Trevor eyed her. "I envy you."

"Why's that?" Mattie paused and looked up from her meal.

He laughed. "You just take everything in stride! I worry about everything. And I do mean every little thing."

Mattie picked up her fork again. "I mean, if there's nothing I can do about something, I'm just gonna keep moving forward. No sense in dwelling when there's other shit to do."

"I don't think sense has anything to do with it," said Trevor. "On either count."

Mattie popped her last bite into her mouth and pondered his words. "Well, I'm not going to worry about it," she said at last.

"Exactly," said Trevor with a wry smile.

Mattie stood and carried her dishes back into the kitchen, rinsing the plate and fork and depositing them in the sink. She reached up and snagged two travel mugs from a shelf above her head, handing one to Trevor and pouring the rest of her own tea into the other. "Let's get moving. I'm sure Tillie will want to be involved in your rehashing and there's no point in doing it twice."

***

Tillie stood under the shower spray, trying to rinse her troubles away. This strategy proved ineffective, but she still felt a little better when she finished. She dried off and wrapped her body in a soft silk robe, her hair in an old cotton t-shirt to ward off the frizz.

She hurried back to her bedroom and opened her closet, considering her options. After a moment, she selected a full skirt that fell to her knees and a scoop-necked blouse that tucked in. Easy to move in, but still classy. And that blue top made her eyes pop.

Tillie smiled and got dressed, selecting a pair of kitten heels to accompany the outfit. She unwrapped her hair from its wrap and walked back to the bathroom to dry and curl it.

As she finished fixing her hair, Tillie reached for her make-up bag and then hesitated. Better not. Not if she was supposed to be pretending to be Mattie.

She compromised again, but managed to do a little less than the day before – she put on lip gloss and nothing else. Surely even her frumpy sister wore lip gloss sometimes, right? And it's not like anyone in St. Louis even knew Mattie anymore.

Tillie heard a knock at the condo door and she hurried out into the living room to open it. There was still no sign of Giovani, who she had ensconced in her guest room for a nap just a few hours ago upon their return from the late-night diner run.

She flung open the door. "Hello!" she said. She gave Trevor an enthusiastic kiss on the cheek and hugged her sister, then stepped back, ushering them inside and closing the door behind them with a perky thump. "Have you guys eaten?"

"Yes, thanks," said Mattie.

"Great!" said Tillie. She walked into the kitchen, calling over her shoulder, "I'll just make myself a smoothie. Would you mind checking on Giovani? He's in the guest room and I'm not sure if he's awake yet."

"He's what?" Mattie yelped.

Oh, right. In all the excitement, Tillie had somehow managed to forget that Giovani had gone missing and that she probably should have told someone that she'd found him.

Oh, well. "He's in the guest room," she repeated. "Turned out he got himself locked in my ritual room."

"Sure," said Trevor. "Like you do."

"Has he attacked you?" asked Mattie.

Tillie frowned as she pulled some fruit from her freezer. "No. Why would he do that?"

She grabbed some oat milk from the fridge, and combined it with the fruit, assembling it all in the blender.

Mattie appeared in the doorway. "Are you serious? Why didn't you bring him to the convent? He needs to be locked up with the rest of them."

"Locked up?" Tillie stared at her sister. "Don't be ridiculous. Why would we lock him up?"

She heard someone knock on the guest room door and it opened.

"Hi," said Giovani's voice, just before Tillie turned on the blender, drowning out all other sounds.

She felt a hand on her shoulder and turned to face her sister, who was studying her face with an air of serious concern. Tillie sighed and turned off the blender. "What?"

Mattie put the back of her hand on Tillie's forehead.

Tillie frowned at her. "What the hell are you doing?"

"We'd better get going now," said Mattie. Her voice echoed the worry etched across her furrowed brow. "You really don't remember what's been going on, do you?"

Tillie frowned back. "I think – I know there's something…. Something about a dream?"

Mattie nodded. "Yes. A dream and . . . ?"

Tillie thought for a second. "Eyes."

"Yes," Mattie nodded emphatically. "What about the eyes?"

"I don't . . ." Tillie squeezed her eyes shut, trying to remember. It was right there, but she couldn't chase down the memory. She opened her eyes again, and Mattie jumped backward with a startled cry.

"Fuck!" said Mattie. "Fuck, fuck, fuck."

"What is it?" asked Tillie urgently. She remembered Giovani having some kind of reaction to her eyes the night before, but she couldn't quite recall that incident in full either.

Mattie grabbed her hand and dragged her out into the living room, where Giovani and Trevor stood, dressed almost identically.

"Wait, so everyone has been doing this? And their eyes did what, exactly?" Giovani was saying.

"We gotta go," Mattie interrupted. "Tillie's eyes . . . flickered."

"Oh, shit," said Trevor. "Did you take a look at her energy?"

Mattie paused, dropping Tillie's hand. "I didn't think of that." She turned toward Tillie. "You must have a scrying stone, right?"

Tillie clinked, confused by the sudden change in topic. Since when could Mattie scry? "Um. Yeah, of course. In there." She pointed toward the linen closet and the secret door to her ritual room.

As she took a step toward the desk where she kept the amulet that opened the door, the heavy antique desk suddenly crashed to the floor on its side, files, pens, and other desky things spilling out of its drawers.

Tillie heard Trevor cry out, and she spun on her heel to find that the tableau behind her had changed in an instant.

Trevor was on the ground, Mattie standing protectively in front of him, hands glowing, shields up.

Giovani stood facing them, completely motionless, the entirety of his eyes flooded with a deep, eerie black that made Tillie's skin crawl.

The key to her ritual room was crawling away from the contents of its drawer, inching itself along the floor, toward the ritual room door.

She flipped her eyes into seer mode and watched it open the room on its own, watched Giovani fly backward into the room as though shoved by a giant hand, and then the door slam shut on its own.

In the present, Tillie launched herself across the room to intercept the amulet, seizing the chain it hung from. It was blazing hot, and she gasped as she dropped it, shaking her hand and whimpering.

The key continued on its way.

Tillie glared at it. Was it somehow jauntier now? The smug bastard of an inanimate object. She spun around to see if Mattie or Trevor were available to help.

Giovani now seemed to be fighting off an invisible enemy, just like in his dream from the day before. He and his assailant moved in unearthly silence, as though they were behind a sound shield. She could see his mouth moving as though he was speaking, but she heard nothing.

Mattie's hands glowed, but Tillie couldn't tell what kind of spell she was doing. Nothing seemed to be affecting Giovani's situation.

Trevor had his hands lifted as though he was going to stitch, but they were motionless and uncertainty was written across his face.

"Hey!" Tillie called. "One of you see if you can help Giovani. The other, come help me with this!"

"Stitch him somewhere," said Mattie to Trevor. "That's helped before." She headed toward Tillie, the glow of her hands fading. "What's going on here?"

Tillie pointed to the amulet, which had reached the linen closet and was climbing upward toward the sunken mage-lock. "We have to stop that from opening the door. I don't know why it keeps trying to shove Giovani in there, but I know I don't want it to succeed."

Mattie reached for it, but Tillie grabbed her arm. "It's hot."

"I'll try a spell," said Mattie. Her hands glowed and the key stopped moving. "Well, that was eas—"

Suddenly, the amulet shot away from the wall and smacked Mattie in the forehead. She swayed slightly and then crumpled to the ground.

Tillie rushed to her sister's side, feeling her neck for a pulse. She sighed in relief as Mattie's blood jumped beneath her fingers.

Then her spine stiffened as she realized that she should have seen this coming. Her seer sight was on, but the future still showed the amulet hanging on the wall, stopped by Mattie's spell. Looking around wildly, Tillie couldn't find it at all in the present, only the future, and the future was clearly false.

"What the *fuck* is going on here?" Tillie yelled, her voice uncharacteristically shrill.

She jumped to her feet, twisting and turning to look for the amulet. The ritual room door hadn't begun to move, so it hadn't reached its goal. And Giovani was still struggling against his invisible assailant, despite Trevor desperately trying stitch after stitch.

Her breathing began to speed up and her heart raced as she tried to focus on one problem, just one thing she could fix. Her eyes fell on Mattie's still unconscious form. Maybe she could stitch her awake.

Tillie fell to her knees again next to her sister and focused on evening out her breath. She needed to concentrate – she'd never used stitching to heal before, and stitching had always been the most difficult form of magery for her.

She lifted her hands and tried to picture the book she'd read that had walked her through the process of healing through magery. She moved her hands in the gesture she hoped was correct.

Instead of Mattie waking up, the desk behind her slid across the room.

"Dammit!" Tillie took a deep breath and prepared to try again. "It's that ring finger angle," she muttered.

"Just slide it underneath." She moved her hands again. This time, Mattie stirred slightly, but she subsided without waking up.

"You've almost got it," Tillie whispered to herself. "Third time's the charm."

She moved her fingers in a complicated pattern.

And everything went dark.

***

Mattie sat up groggily and looked around, hoping that she'd been out for a while and things had been taken care of.

Nope. Giovani was still grappling with some unseen, unheard enemy. Trevor was rushing around, trying to stitch at them from various angles with no luck. And Tillie was passed out right next to her. What the hell had happened to her?

Mattie leaned over to check that her sister was breathing and then jumped to her feet. Where was the amulet? It was really important that she stop it from doing whatever the hell it was trying to do.

She spotted it, still creeping up the wall, almost to the spot where it would fit in and open the door. "Oh, hell, no," she told it. "I can't use a spell on you? No problem."

Aiming her hands toward the door, she formed a spell in her head and gouged a huge dent right where the key fit in, altering the shape of the indentation. "Let's see how you open your precious secret room now, shitsucker."

The key paused, bobbing comically, as though it was looking around for a way out. Then it seemed to sag in defeat and dropped to the ground.

A grunt sounded from behind her, and Mattie spun around to see what was going on.

Giovani's wide eyes stared at her, the whites white and his irises back to their natural light brown. He swayed, blinked, and keeled over sideways.

Trevor rushed to catch him but only managed to slow his fall a little with his arms, as Giovani crashed to the ground, narrowly missing the corner of the coffee table.

"Are you okay?" asked Trevor, kneeling and gently flipping Giovani over.

Giovani just moaned.

"Let's get him to the couch," suggested Mattie. She bent to support him on one side, while Trevor did the same on the other,

With Giovani's arms slung over their shoulders, the three of them staggered over to the sofa and got the former Auditor comfortable.

Then Mattie turned her attention back to her twin. "Can you stitch her awake?" she asked Trevor.

"I don't know," he said doubtfully. "I think that's what she was trying to do for you and then she blacked out."

"Oh, shit."

"How did you get knocked out, anyway?" Trevor asked. "You weren't in the weird black-eye-dream-space were you?"

She shook her head. "No, I just got conked in the head."

"Ah," said Trevor. "The old-fashioned way of passing out."

"I'd have preferred drinking too much tequila," said Mattie.

"Well, you can't win 'em all." Trevor grinned. His smile faded almost immediately as he lowered himself down to the floor next to Tillie. "So, if there was nothing magical about your situation, why did trying to reverse it knock her out?"

Tillie sat up, suddenly, and Trevor jerked back.

"What happened?" shouted Tillie. "Is everyone okay?"

Trevor rolled his eyes at her. "You're the one who wasn't okay, Tills. You fainted."

"Oh." Tillie stared at him and then looked at Mattie and Giovani sitting on the couch. "So, everything's good now?"

"I don't know about that," said Mattie. She turned to Giovani. "Can you shed any light on what the hell happened, bud? One minute you were sitting quietly, listening to Trevor talk, and the next your eyes went black, but you weren't behaving the way the others had."

"Let me guess," said Giovani, grimly. "I was fighting someone invisible."

"Yeah." Mattie narrowed her eyes. "You were aware of it?"

"Sort of." Giovani filled them in on what had happened to him the day before.

When he was done, Mattie sat in stunned silence, absorbing it all. She glanced at Tillie. Her sister didn't seem terribly surprised – he must have already told her all of this.

"So, why is your experience completely different than everyone else's?" asked Trevor. "I think we need to take a look at your energy fields."

"Tillie's too," Mattie reminded him.

"Let's get you two to the convent and move you to the front of the line," said Trevor grimly.

***

Tillie tried to listen as Sister Regina explained to her and the others who hadn't been there what they'd seen the night before in Nicole and Danielle's energy systems. Her attention kept wandering, which felt very strange – she'd always been an extremely focused person.

She found herself transfixed by Sister Regina's crooked nun-head-thingy. Finally, she couldn't take it anymore. Maybe she'd be able to listen to the woman if she was dressed properly.

Tillie got to her feet and strode up to the front of the classroom, taking the headdress – no, the word started with a w, didn't it? – and gently pulled free the pins holding it in place, straightened it out on her head, and tucked the pins back in.

Then she drifted back to her seat and set her chin on her hand, prepared to really listen now.

She frowned. How had it gotten crooked again? She was sure she'd fixed it properly in place.

Tillie stood up again and walked back up to Sister Regina, who just kept talking, blah, blah, toxic energy, blah, blah, blah. She straightened the wimple – that was the word! – again and sat back down.

It was back to crooked again. What the hell?

***

Mattie waited patiently as Sister Regina filled in the others of the group on the situation with their allies' energy systems, keeping one eye on her sister and Giovani. They had collectively decided that since the pair of them were behaving completely differently than the others, it might behoove them to study them first, rather than tossing them into a cell.

Frowning, Mattie studied Tillie's side profile. She didn't seem to be listening at all, just sat there, her posture uncharacteristically slumped. Something was definitely wrong.

Mattie nudged Trevor, who sat next to her, and nodded toward Tillie when he glanced over.

He pursed his lips and dug in his pocket, pulling out a quarter and handing it to Mattie.

Mattie couldn't help but grin. In elementary school, whenever her attention was wandering, Trevor or Tillie would throw coins at her to get her to focus on the teacher.

She held out her hand for the quarter and Trevor placed it in her palm.

Taking careful aim, Mattie flicked her wrist, tossing the coin like a tiny frisbee.

It hit Tillie on the shoulder. She straightened slowly and turned her head toward Mattie. Her eyes were full of darkness.

Mattie's grin faded and Trevor let out a wordless shout of dismay.

Tillie's eyes began flickering back and forth between black and normal, as though the spell was fighting her for control.

Trevor's fingers moved in a stitching gesture, and Tillie blinked out from her seat and into the next chair over. Her eyes were normal as she turned her head from side to side, clearly disoriented.

"What's going on?" Tillie asked. She glanced up toward the head of the classroom and frowned. "How is it still crooked?" she muttered.

Mattie couldn't believe her ears. Tillie was seriously worried about Sister Regina's wimple at a time like this? She walked over to her sister and leaned down in front of her, peering into her eyes for any sign of flickering blackness. "We'd better get started checking out Tillie's whatchamacallits."

"Meridians and chakras," said Sister Regina coldly.

"Right," said Mattie. "Enough chatting about it. Let's get this hippy shit show on the road."

Sister Regina muttered something inaudible under her breath, but she obligingly pulled her scrying stone out of a beige tote bag with the name of the school on it and set it down on a desk in the center of the room. "I'll take the first shift of scrying today," she said aloud.

That suited Mattie fine – she was in no rush to repeat the headache of the day before.

Instead, she positioned herself behind Sister Regina, readying the spell to project the scene from the scrying stone onto the white poster board that Father Sean held up.

Sister Regina switched her eyes into seer mode and Mattie watched as tiny images appeared in the stone. She couldn't see them clearly, the way she could when she was the one doing the seeing, but she set her spell. Her hands began to glow and the images appeared, large and easy to see. She adjusted the view so that only Tillie and Trevor, who was standing next to her, showed up.

Tillie's figure wasn't actually all that different from Trevor's. Where his energy was made of golden light, Tillie's looked sort of pus-colored, and dark blue lines ran across the rivers, blocking the flow. The chakras moved more slowly than Trevor's, but the colors were only a little muted, and they weren't nearly as erratic as Nicole's and Danielle's had been.

"Well, that's not so bad," said Sister Catherine. She stood up and studied the image. "I'm guessing the others were worse?"

"Much worse," said Father Sean. "Do you think you can fix this one?"

"Absolutely," said Sister Catherine. "Assuming it'll let me."

"Why is hers so much less, I wonder?" said Father Sean.

"I have a better question," said Sister Helen. "Why is she affected at all? You were never actually part of the organization at all, were you, Tillie?"

Tillie shook her head. "I infiltrated the local HQ for a few days. That's all."

Sister Catherine cocked her head, studying Tillie's projected energy systems. Then she began to move her hands, combing the air in front of the picture, following the lines of Tillie's energy with crooked fingers.

The areas in front of Sister Catherine's fingers brightened, still not matching the warm gold of Trevor's, but not looking quite so infected. Then she reached one of the blue blocks and her fingers stopped as thought stuck. She seemed to be straining against a physical barrier.

Finally, she dropped her hands, her breathing heavy.

Trevor took her arm and guided her gently to a chair.

"Thank you," said Sister Catherine, finally catching her breath. "I thought I was making progress, but those blockades just aren't moving."

Sister Helen stood and took the place Sister Catherine had been standing. She reached forward and gently traced along the image of Tillie's energy, more slowly than Sister Catherine had.

As before, the colors changed, growing more healthy-looking, as she did so. When she reached the first of the blue things, she didn't try to budge it.

Instead, she began poking and prodding at the air, looking for all the world as though there was a cat toy hanging in front of her and she was trying to bat at it. She bunched her fingers together and then spread them out, as though enlarging something on a tablet screen.

"It's working!" said Trevor.

Sure enough, the blue object lodged in Tillie's energetic artery was starting to shrink.

Mattie began to laugh; she wasn't even really sure why. Nothing was funny. She was just so relieved that her sister had escaped another terrible fate.

Sister Helen didn't speak. She just continued her minute adjustments until finally the blue blockade was completely gone and the light was flowing strongly toward the next chakra.

The room erupted into cheers.

Finally, Sister Helen looked up, smiling gently. "I'm glad to help," she said. "But don't cheer just yet." She held up a finger and counted the rest of the blockages. "There are still six more here. And that's just Tillie. It sounds like the others are worse off, right?"

Mattie sighed. Nothing was ever simple when magic was involved.

"We should split up again," suggested Sister Timothy Ann. "One seer, one speller, one stitcher per group."

"We have four stitchers here," said Trevor. "Three spellers, and only two seers. Not counting Tillie and Giovani, of course."

"I can help," said Giovani. "After you fix me. And so can Tillie."

"And either of us can fill in as a speller," Tillie pointed out. She sounded more like herself, Mattie noted, a note of confidence in her voice that had been missing for the past couple of days.

Sister Helen had resumed stitching, working on another block.

"You've got another speller right here," said a tired voice from the doorway. Ida slowly walked into the room, leaning against a cane. The cane was made of dark wood and was carved to resemble a sinuous dragon, her hand resting on its head, its rubber-tipped tail thumping against the tile floor with each step.

Mattie met Trevor's eyes, troubled. She shook her head. There was no stopping Ida Garaveldi if she didn't want to be stopped. Still, the projection spell wasn't difficult. The old woman should be able to handle it, right?

She eyed Ida uncertainly. She'd never seen her with a cane. Then again, she hadn't known her for that long. Maybe she used a cane regularly and had just been feeling particularly spry for the past few weeks.

"All right," said Sister Catherine. "Mattie, Sister Regina, and Sister Helen, since you're already working on Tillie, you'll continue as a team."

Mattie sighed inwardly. Well, maybe she could swap out Sister Regina for Tillie once they'd finished with her.

Sister Catherine continued, quickly assigning all of the teams. She put Tillie with Ida and Father Bruce, dashing Mattie's hopes of switching seers. That made sense, though, actually. She was probably figuring that would give Ida more downtime to rest.

As most of the group left the room, heading down to the dungeon to see if they could help their confined allies, Mattie turned her attention back to Tillie.

Sister Helen had already managed to get two more blockages fixed. She was almost halfway done.

***

Tillie was feeling more energized than she had in days. A fog was lifting and memories were gradually starting to return to her as well. She remembered yesterday's meeting about the spell that had been placed upon the former Auditor agents. She recalled how and why she had been looking for Giovani, and why she had been planning to bring him in before they got distracted by diner food.

She realized that the spell had somehow been affecting her and that it was going away. She felt like she was breathing properly again, for the first time since she'd gotten into Giovani's car the night before and had lost her voice.

Tillie's attention wandered over to Giovani, who stood stiffly on the other side of the room as Sister Margaret arranged her scrying supplies in front of him and Trevor and Father Sean waited patiently for their parts.

Tillie found herself mesmerized by Sister Margaret's lithe movements and shapely curves. If only she wasn't a nun…. She tore her gaze away, only to find her sister smirking at her.

"She belongs to Jesus," Mattie mouthed at her. "You should be ashamed of yourself."

Tillie rolled her eyes. "I wasn't going to do anything about it," she murmured. "But I can't help having eyes."

Mattie laughed.

Sister Margaret happened to glance over at them just then, and Tillie could feel her face heating up. She needed to get ahold of her libido and fast.

She hurriedly looked away, only to find Giovani's eyes darting from her face to Sister Margaret's. Tillie winced. So much for professional discretion and subtly.

Whatever. She and Giovani were just friends, right? So, why did she suddenly feel guilty?

Tillie forced herself to focus on Sister Regina, who was fortunately not someone she would ever be attracted to.

Sister Regina was somehow managing to scry and glare at Tillie over her scrying stone at the same time.

She was probably a math teacher. Tillie had never done well in math.

Desperate to distract herself with anything unrelated to her own libido, Tillie flipped her eyes into seer mode and focused on the halls of the school, beyond the room she stood in.

Summer had just started, so only a couple of rooms were occupied.

She watched in one room as a woman taught three bored teens the basics of biology. Summer school probably – these would be the students who had failed the class during the regular school year.

Tillie moved on down the hall and found a room where four girls and one adult were enthusiastically discussing the merits of various musicals. Drama club, she assumed. Probably picking the theatrical line-up for the next school year.

With effort, Tillie pushed her focus further away. It was difficult to go so far without a scrying stone, but she was proud of her ability to do so.

Down the hall from the drama club, Tillie found the music room. This was more like it. She listened raptly as a talented teen worked her way through a beautiful Bach piece on a viola.

Just as the girl was finishing the sonata, Tillie felt a hand on her shoulder. She jumped, startled back to the room her body was occupying. "Hi," she said, giving Mattie a rueful smile and moving out of seer mode. "Sorry. Just needed to distract myself."

"We're all done now," said Sister Regina briskly. "You're cured. Probably."

7.

Mattie released her projection spell and then stretched her arms as high as she could, using the momentum of the stretch to stumble the few steps to the nearest chair. She flung herself down and closed her eyes. Maybe Trevor had a point – she wouldn't do anyone any good if she burnt herself out again. "I don't know about anyone else, but I need a break," she said.

She glanced at the clock. It had taken over two hours to remove the effects of the spell on Tillie's energy body. And did they even know that it would actually be effective in removing the actual spell?

"We can take a few minutes," said Sister Regina. The nun sounded like she was doing everyone else a favor, but there was definite weariness in her voice.

Turning her attention to the other team in the room, Mattie watched as Trevor and Father Bruce worked together on Giovani's heart chakra. Their fingers moved quickly as they manipulated the spinning disk, first setting it so that it only spun in one direction and then regulating its speed to the normal lazy rotation.

Mattie studied Giovani's image on the poster board, maintained by Father Sean's glowing hands.

Father Sean sat behind Sister Margaret, one hand on her shoulder, linking his spell to her seeing, and the other resting in his lap. His eyes were closed as he concentrated.

To Mattie's far-from-expert assessment, Giovani's energy system was somewhere between Danielle's and Nicole's in severity. Not the pure congealed black of Nicole's, but somehow still worse than Danielle's.

And they'd been working for a good hour and a half. Maybe it had started out as bad as Nicole's.

Mattie scanned the floor, looking for the water bottle she'd left beside the chair she'd been sitting in earlier. Oh, there it was, next to Father Sean's chair; he must have taken it.

She got up to grab it, accidentally bumping the middle-aged priest's ankle as she picked it up. It made an odd clunking noise, and she realized with a start that it was a prosthetic. Well, that explained his limp.

Mattie's already-high opinion of Father Sean rose as she thought back to how well he'd fought in the battle the week before.

She returned to her own chair, sipping on water, doing her best to refill her energy reserves. There was still plenty of work to be done, and she was finding it more difficult than she expected to force herself to rest.

Maybe she hadn't grown as much as she thought. She should probably apologize to Trevor at some point.

Abruptly, Sister Regina broke the comfortable silence that had filled the classroom. "Ida Garaveldi is your aunt." It was phrased like a statement, but the question was clearly there and addressed to Giovani.

"Yes," said Giovani. He looked as startled by the interruption as Mattie felt.

Her eyes fixed themselves on his face, searching for something. "The Pontiff was your cousin, then."

He squirmed a little under her regard. "I mean, we weren't raised together or anything…."

"Please don't fidget," said Father Bruce.

Giovani took in a deep breath and returned to his stiff pose with visible effort.

"Hey, that's weird," said Mattie. "He must have known about you, right? At some point, he had to have learned that there was an Agent Garaveldi brought in. If he did a little digging, he would have seen that you were from St. Louis, just like his parents."

"It's not a common surname," Tillie pointed out.

"There are thousands of Auditors," said Giovani. "Why would he have noticed one out of thousands, across the world, just because I had the same last name as his mom? The man has never even spoken to me. I never even saw him until I'd been in the organization for years already."

Suddenly, Mattie remembered something. "Tillie. Remember when the Pontiff asked you to deliver that message when you were posing as an agent?"

"Uh, yeah," said Tillie. "What about it?"

"He was surprised by your name."

Tillie frowned. "And he said he didn't know of an Agent Holiday stationed in St. Louis."

"So he does learn names," said Sister Regina triumphantly. She jumped to her feet and pointed at Giovani. "There's something special about your whole spell situation, and it has something to do with your relatedness to the Pontiff! That's why you're fighting a strange enemy instead of attacking the people around you, and it has to be why you heard the Pontiff's voice."

Trevor paused in his task, turning to regard Sister Regina. "Need I remind you all that the Pontiff is dead?"

"So?" Sister Regina spun around to study him in turn. "What does that have to do with the price of tea in China?"

Mattie threw up her hands in exasperation. "So, this spell can't have been his doing! It would have faded as soon as he died!"

"Let's get logical about this," suggested Tillie, striding to the front of the room and picking up a piece of chalk. She began busily making a table on the board, with columns for *Giovani, Not Giovani,* and *Everyone.* "Okay, so what have we seen so far from this spell?"

Trevor returned to helping Father Bruce with Giovani's energy system, but Mattie noticed that he adjusted his position to keep half an eye on the chalkboard too.

"Black eyes," said Father Sean, lifting his head and regarding the board with interest.

Tillie wrote it under *Everyone.*

"Weird dreams," said Mattie.

Tillie gestured toward Mattie with her chalk. "Yes, but more specifically, everyone has had the dream of the Pontiff visiting and spelling them during their training period."

She wrote *Pontiff Spell Dream* on the board under *Everyone* and then gestured toward Giovani. "And you've had the one where you're fighting someone you can't see."

She wrote *Unseen Enemy Dream* under *Giovani.*

"That one isn't a dream," Mattie objected. "It seems to be actually happening, bruises and all."

"Yeah, but the setting changes," said Giovani. "It's only happened when I've been in Tillie's condo, but I'm transported to a motel room each time."

"What's significant about the motel room?" asked Trevor.

Giovani shrugged. "Familiarity? I've spent a lot of time in motel rooms as an Auditor agent."

"If the Pontiff – or whoever – wanted to create a constructed experience to trigger in someone, a motel room is a good choice," said Sister Regina.

Mattie leaned forward. "Explain that."

"It requires a seer, a speller, and a stitcher," said Father Sean. "Or someone who can do all three, but they'd have to be very powerful to pull it off alone."

"It's like a virtual reality simulator," said Sister Regina.

"We use the technique sometimes to treat veterans or anyone else with PTSD," said Father Sean. "Before all of this happened, I was actually considering using it to help the former Auditors with their brainwashing."

Oh, right. Mattie remembered that Father Sean was a psychiatrist or something.

"That's very interesting," said Tillie. "But why would they create that constructed experience about the Pontiff?"

Sister Regina shrugged. "It could also be a side effect of the spell."

"So, you're saying we still don't know shit." Mattie sighed and stared at the board. "Let's keep thinking. Get it all up there and maybe we'll see a pattern."

Just then, Ida hobbled into the room, still leaning heavily on her cane. "Ah, good. You've finished with Tillie."

"How are you feeling?" said Mattie, vacating her chair near the door and moving to another further away.

Ida waved a hand airily. "Oh, you know, just a little bit tired today. I'll be just fine." She did take the chair, though.

"We're just trying to get to the bottom of why Giovani's spell is different," said Tillie, indicating the table on the board.

Ida's eyes were sharp as she studied the chart. "Well, he's a Garaveldi," she said proudly. "Of course he's different. Better, I would think."

"Well," said Sister Regina with an eye-roll. "I don't know about better, but yes, we think it's because he's related to the Pontiff."

"You think that," said Tillie. "I'm not convinced."

Ida studied Sister Regina, drumming her fingers on the top of her cane. "Never did care much for your grandmother, Cassie Cambell. And your mother was a bad seed too. I was glad to see you going in a different direction, but maybe I was wrong. Maybe you're just as bad. The apple doesn't fall far from the tree, I always say."

Sister Regina's lips tightened and she sucked in a sharp breath through her nose before replying. "It's Sister Regina now. I'll thank you not to refer to me as Cassie."

"Ah, yes," said Ida. "Very humble, taking a name that means *queen*. You think you're very regal, I suppose. Well, I didn't spend sixty years—"

"It refers to the Virgin Mary!" Sister Regina snapped.

Mattie jumped to her feet, readying a shield spell to go up in between the arrogant nun and Ida's inevitable wrath at being interrupted. These two were much too similar to be in the same room together.

But Ida just sighed and shook her head. "Your family always was too big for its britches."

"Huh," Sister Regina muttered. "Says a Garaveldi."

"Enough!" Mattie strode across the room to stand between the feuding mages. "You're both . . . delightfully confident. Let's leave it at that. Now, we need to solve this puzzle before it gets worse."

Tillie turned to Ida. "How are things going downstairs?"

"Slowly." Her arms were still folded tightly across her chest and she kept glancing angrily at Sister Regina. "They're making some headway on Danielle. Nicole is about as bad as Danielle was to start with now, I suppose. You can't measure something without a good comparison, though, I always say. Maybe it's going quickly, compared to something else."

Sister Regina was drumming her fingers on her desk in an irritating and constant pattern, over and over again. *Tap-tap tap tap-tap-tap.*

Mattie formed a silence shield spell in her mind and sent it toward Sister Regina's fingers.

The nun's lips pursed and she did another one of her sharp nose breaths, looking around to see who had set the spell, her eyes narrowing at the sight of Mattie's glowing hands. Mattie smirked at her and turned her attention back to the group.

"I feel a lot better," said Tillie. "Better than I have in ages. Like I've just taken a bunch of vitamins and then worked out. Full of endorphins and vitality."

"So, I think we can tentatively say that it's working," said Trevor. "At least on our first subject. And maybe it's smaller because she was only nominally part of the organization. If she'd stayed, she might have ended up like all the others."

"But what's different about Giovani?" asked Tillie. "He's not like all the others."

"His connection to the Pontiff!" said Sister Regina. "That's the only extenuating circumstance."

"I feel like we're just going around and around in circles," said Father Sean.

A thought occurred to Mattie, and she leaped up. "That's it! We have to stop worrying about this and get back to what we were doing before – plotting to take down the Auditors."

Silence fell over the room as everyone stared at her with puzzled looks on their faces. Even Father Bruce and Sister Margaret turned to look at her.

Mattie shook her head. "Listen. We're going about this all wrong. What is the point of this spell?"

Tillie's eyebrows shot up. "She's right. It's a distraction. We're spending way too much time dealing with something that isn't even particularly problematic."

"Not problematic?" said Giovani. "I call having my mind taken over very problematic, actually."

She nodded. "Yours, yes. But the others' spell is easy to deal with, even if we aren't able to break it. You just stitch them to a foot away, and they're fine. Since it's easy to fix, it must be meant only as a distraction. But from what?"

Suddenly, an alarm was going off, a shrill klaxon of sirens.

"The prisoners," said Sister Margaret, grimly. "The real prisoners."

"You mean . . . ?" said Mattie.
"The court is breaking free."

8.

Tillie rushed after everyone else toward the dungeons in the basement. "We have to free the others first," she called, as the rest of the group turned toward the stairs that would lead to the higher security cells where the court was being kept.

Without waiting for a response, Tillie sprinted in the other direction, shoving a member of the drama club out of her way as the students also emerged from their classroom to see what was going on. She kicked off her kitten heels and stitched in a pair of comfortable flats as she ran, pausing to put them on as soon as they appeared in her hand.

The sirens stopped and in the sudden silence, she could hear running footsteps catching up with her. She hoped it was Mattie and Trevor and not a bunch of untrained theatre kids – she'd had enough of that dealing with Sammy.

Tillie reached the door to the stairwell and wrenched open the door, flipping on her seer sight as she did so. It was Mattie and Trevor behind her, she realized as she saw Mattie overtake and pass her in the next few minutes. She stepped aside to let her by and then grabbed Trevor's hand. "Can you stitch us down there?" she asked. "I'm too tired for something that big."

Suddenly, they were in front of the first of the former Auditors' cells. It was already empty. That made sense – Ida had mentioned that the other two teams had been working on Nicole and Danielle.

They'd probably already all headed out when the sirens had gone off.

Without missing a beat, Tillie ran to the next cell and flung open the door, inwardly thanking the nuns for using spells to keep them locked on the inside but not the outside. This would have taken much longer if they had to mess around with keys or something.

"The shit's hitting the fan!" she yelled. "Let's go!"

She held the door open for the pair of mages inside and then rushed to the next cell. Down the corridor, she could see Trevor opening other rooms, and the two she had just freed pushed past her to help out with the further ones.

With each group adding to their crew of door-openers, they had everyone out within just a few minutes.

"This way!" she called and sprinted past the confused, milling mages to lead them toward the area where the court was being kept. Her seer sight showed them following her.

It was only a short way to the main dungeon section, where the cells were smaller and less comfortable and had to be opened by someone specifically keyed to the lock.

The cells were empty.

The hallway, however, was full of people. Sister Margaret was at the head of a group of about twenty nuns. Ida and Fathers Bruce and Sean were also there.

Ida held her cane in one hand and was levitating a couple inches above the floor instead of leaning on it.

Tillie spared a moment to wonder if Ida should really be participating in this. She dismissed the concern as pointless – she certainly wasn't going to tell Ida Garaveldi what she couldn't do and she doubted anyone else would either.

Tillie focused her attention on what Sister Margaret was saying.

"Ah, I see we have reinforcements. Excellent. I know you're all still under this spell – let's all just remember that if an ally attacks you, it appears that any stitchers around can stop them simply by stitching them to a new position. We'll have at least one person on each team who can stitch and isn't prone to going black-eyed.

"For those of you just arriving, I'll summarize the plan. Teams of four, representing at least one of each discipline. Dividing up the building into sections. Each team will search their section. If you finish your section and don't find anything, you will start over. Keep searching just your section until you either find someone or you get word to stop. This will prevent us from missing a prisoner who is moving around the property to avoid us. If you do find someone, you'll text Sister Helen, who won't be on a team and will come to fetch your prisoner. Then you'll go back to your sweep.

"Remember, as soon as the alarms went off, the barrier spell went up. This is one of the strongest spells the Sister of Saint Joan have. No one can get in or out of the entire property. That includes stitching, walking, flying, or digging. It's a complete sphere, and it's keyed to every sister in our order, present or not, so it'll last until it's either switched off or all of us are dead and not in a position to give a fuck about the spell anymore.

"Other things that happened when the alarms went off: any kind of illusion spell was disabled. So, even if you're not a seer, you can see right through any sight shields, sound shields, or disguise spells. A silent alarm went out to our order's main office in Jefferson City. They'll be monitoring the situation and send back-up if they feel like we need it. And, finally, trap spells are scattered throughout the building. Anyone who walks into one and isn't wearing some representation of our order's symbol will set off the trap."

Sister Margaret unzipped her tight leather sleeve to show the crowd a large tattoo on her forearm that depicted a stylized flaming sword. "Don't worry, it doesn't have to be a tattoo. As we assign teams, Sister Catherine will be handing out talismans for you to wear around your neck."

Tillie was impressed, even more than when she'd seen the facilities in the first place, just after the battle, when they'd brought the court prisoners here. This place took security seriously.

She waited as Sister Margaret began assigning teams and territories. Finally, it was her turn. She ended up on a team with Trevor, Giovani, and Father Sean.

Father Sean was given a large card with a map of the building and a particular area highlighted.

All three of them were given necklaces with the flaming sword symbol.

It was a good team. Tillie and Father Sean were highly skilled mages who would probably be able to contain Giovani if he went black-eyed – definitely a factor since he was the only one that the stitching thing didn't seem to work on. Trevor's lack of experience was made up for in raw power and good sense. And Giovani, well, assuming he remained in possession of his own mind, he was one of the best mages they had.

Sister Margaret was coming to the end of the group, but something was wrong – there was a commotion down the hall.

Tillie craned her neck to see better.

It had something to do with the last two rebel agents she had brought in the day before from the HQ site.

Pushing her way back down the hall, Tillie managed to get into hearing distance.

"She was right here," Bernie was saying. "Literally a minute ago."

"Who?" Tillie asked.

"Polly," said Bernie, turning to face her. "My wife. She was here and then this lady started assigning teams and I turned to say something about how I hoped we'd be on the same team, and she was gone."

Sister Margaret hissed in frustration. "We'll have to redo the teams. I divided you into fours because the number we had was divisible by four."

Tillie shrugged. "Just have one team of three. I'm more concerned about Polly. Either she turned coat, which could be this black-eye spell or it could mean she's a traitor, or she's lost. Either way, it's concerning."

"Our priority has to be the court prisoners," said Sister Margaret.

Bernie opened his mouth as though to protest, but Sister Margaret lifted a hand to forestall his argument. "I'm sorry. I know it's not ideal, but I'm in charge of the security of this facility, and that's the way it has to be. I will, however, assign your team to a nearby area, so that you're most likely to find her if she's just wandered off. Okay?"

He nodded, tight-lipped and terse.

"Okay. So that's settled." She beckoned to Sister Regina, who jogged over to them. "I'm giving them your territory, and you can take the area around the school cafeteria."

"Sure." Sister Regina traded map cards with Sister Margaret, who handed the new one to Bernie.

Sister Regina headed back to her team, and Sister Margaret turned to Tillie. "Get back to your team, please. You have a strong group, so you'll be taking the area near the back entrance that the court was brought in through. That's the most logical place for the prisoners to head."

***

Mattie waited patiently as Sister Margaret headed back toward her. She was pleased to be assigned a team with her friend, alongside Ida and Amy.

Amy nudged Mattie. "Hey, listen, I'm really sorry I attacked you and Sister Margaret yesterday."

"Don't worry about it," said Sister Margaret as she arrived at their side. "It's in the past. I forgive you for attacking us if you forgive me for knocking you out with my sword hilt."

"Of course!" said Amy. "I'm just grateful you didn't slit my throat or something."

"Great. We're even. Let's get to the task at hand," said Sister Margaret. "We will be searching this area, around the cells, in case anyone is lingering. We'll stick together." She unsheathed one of her hip-side swords with a deadly *swoosh*, lifting it in her right hand. "Weapons out if you've got them. Defensive spells or stitches ready. Let's start with the inside of the cells. We will also be looking for anything that might show us what their plan is and how they broke out in the first place."

Amy raised a hand tentatively. "We could replay the scenes?"

Mattie sighed internally. She didn't know Amy very well, but what she'd seen was that the woman was but the woman was nice, but timid, which didn't really come in handy in situations like this.

Sister Margaret raised her eyebrows. "Explain that."

"We used to do it sometimes when we were hunting abominations—" she glanced apologetically at Mattie.

Mattie gave her an encouraging smile.

"When I was a field agent, I mean," concluded Amy.

Of course, she hadn't lasted long in the field, getting "promoted" to a station agent position as soon as her superiors had realized she was better suited to sitting in an office.

"Just spit it out, dear," said Ida, not unkindly. "What do you mean 'replay the scenes?'"

Amy gestured toward Sister Margaret. "You have a seer and a stitcher." She gestured toward herself. "The seer looks to the future and the stitcher pulls her into the past. It's easier if you have a speller around too because then you—" she waved toward Ida and Mattie "—can project the scene and it takes less effort for me to see it through the seer's eyes."

"Sounds great," said Sister Margaret.

Amy beamed.

"We should do a sweep of the area first," she continued. "Just to catch any stragglers. Then we'll pick a cell and replay the past couple of days. Can we fast forward through until we get to the good parts?"

"Well, you can only do the past couple of hours," said Amy. "But, yeah, you can adjust the speed."

"Then we'd better hurry up, I suppose," said Ida. She snapped her fingers. "Let's get cracking. No time to waste."

Mattie pushed open the door to the nearest cell, holding it wide for the rest of her team to enter and then following them into the tiny, bare room.

These cells were definitely more what you pictured when someone talked about a prison. The rooms they'd held their allies in had room to move around, furniture, TVs, and separate bathrooms.

The ones the real prisoners were held in contained a single cot against one wall and a toilet in the corner. She did notice that the floors were carpeted and the place was clean. And you couldn't see into them from the hallway like you could the comfy rooms.

Mattie spared a moment to wonder why the other rooms had those giant observation windows. What had the nuns originally intended them for? Then she dismissed the thought as irrelevant and began to look around the sparse cell.

It didn't take long. "There's nothing here," said Sister Margaret. "Let's hit up the next one."

After a few cells, they fell into a rhythm. One person would go into the cell, while the other three watched from the doorway. It was easier than crowding everyone into the tiny rooms.

Without discussion, the group rotated who went in. Occasionally, someone in the doorway would spot something that looked interesting and point it out.

Whoever was inside the room would check it out.

It invariably turned out to be a piece of dropped food or a ripped page from a book – food and books being the only outside objects the prisoners had been given. Oddly enough, other than the first cell, each one seemed to have at least one torn page.

"Barbarians," muttered Mattie the first time she found a page ripped from a book. She got down on her knees to look under the cot.

"Hey, where are the books themselves?" asked Amy from the doorway.

"They must have taken them with them, I suppose," said Ida. "That seems odd, doesn't it? A book would weigh them down and isn't much use as a weapon unless it's a really big one. When you escape from anywhere, take nothing except food and drink, I always say."

Mattie pivoted on her knees to regard Ida, brows raised. "How often have you had occasion to say that?"

Ida smirked at her. "Oh, you'd be surprised how many times I've been locked up in my day."

Mattie laughed. "Maybe I wouldn't." She scooted backward and got to her feet. "It's an interesting question, though. What kind of books did they have?" She picked up the page she'd found to examine it.

It appeared to be science fiction. A character named Jez was gleefully flying a spaceship.

Sister Margaret shrugged. "Whatever they asked for. We're not stingy with books. They'd only get one at a time, but they're free to call for new ones whenever they finish, and they're welcome to whatever books are in our library."

"Let's hold onto the torn page, in case it turns out to matter," said Mattie. "Other than that, I don't see anything in this cell."

"Did every prisoner get books?" asked Amy as the team trooped toward the next cell.

Sister Margaret shook her head. "I have no idea. That's a question for Sister Helen. She's in charge of detention." She pulled out her phone and fired off a text.

The next cell contained a page torn from a Bible, which prompted a long string of rapid Spanish from Sister Margaret – Mattie didn't know a lot of Spanish, but she recognized a couple of curse words.

The cell after that was Shakespeare; as an English teacher, Mattie recognized the sonnets immediately.

By the time they finished the circuit of the twenty-odd cells that had been occupied by court prisoners, Amy was carrying around a stack of thirty-two pages from a seemingly random assortment of books, ranging from genre fiction to a treatise on the mating habits of badgers.

"The really odd thing about this is that these are the books requested by the court," said Amy. "I worked in three different stations and never saw a single fiction book in any of our library rooms."

"All the books I saw in the St. Louis station were about the organization," objected Mattie. "They could hardly have expected to find those books in the convent library."

Amy shook her head. "You must have been in a specific room. The books were scattered throughout the stations, but each room had a theme. There were books about all kinds of subjects, but they were all non-fiction, research-type stuff."

"They were probably starving for something actually interesting, I suppose," said Ida. "I can't stand reading that kind of thing, personally. I was so glad when the internet came around and I didn't have to remember dry facts about anything. I can just look up anything at all whenever I want to. Or at least, I can instruct whatever young person is nearby to do it for me. Modern technology is a godsend, I always say, but I never bothered to learn to use it, myself. That's what you all are for, I suppose. If all I ever had around was boring textbooks and suddenly a nice lady was offering me anything I wanted to read, you bet your bonnet I'd be tearing through historical romance novels before you could say 'bodice ripper.'"

"What about the badger book?" said Mattie.

"Well, there's always someone who's just weird, I suppose." Ida dismissed this with a wave.

Sister Margaret cleared her throat. "Fascinating as this speculation is, let's save it. I'd like to try Amy's idea of replaying the scenes before too much time goes by and there's nothing to see."

"Good call," said Mattie. "Let's start with this cell here, then."

Sister Margaret turned to Amy. "What do I need to do?"

"I don't suppose you have a scrying stone on you?" Amy asked.

Mattie stitched in the stone they'd been using upstairs and handed it to Sister Margaret.

It belonged to Sister Regina, but surely she couldn't object under the circumstances.

"Thank you." Sister Margaret looked around, finally setting the stone down on top of the toilet tank. She sat down backward on the lid of the toilet, legs straddling the tank so she faced the stone.

Good thing it wasn't the standard prison toilet you always saw on TV with no lid.

Amy positioned herself behind Sister Margaret, placing her hands on the seer's shoulders. "Mattie, can you project the image onto the wall?"

"Yep." Mattie turned to face the white cinder block wall, ready to display whatever showed up in the stone.

Ida sat down on the cot. "I'll just take a little rest, then, I suppose."

Mattie glanced over at the elderly speller with concern. Ida sounded tired and *old*. And they had been convinced that today would be okay for her – that there wouldn't be any action.

She shook her head, focusing on the wall again as Sister Margaret began to scry. Nothing to be done. It was all hands on deck right now. She'd make sure Ida got some rest after today, no matter what she said.

As Mattie's hands began to glow, a picture of the cell appeared on the wall, showing the four of them in their current position.

Out of the corner of her eye, she saw Amy's fingers moving against Sister Margaret's shoulders.

Amy's hands started to glow as well, and suddenly the picture on the wall showed only one person in the cell, a woman with a bright orange mohawk, dressed in a black jumpsuit with white piping at the neck, wrists, waist, and ankles, giving the impression that the prisoner was wearing a pajama set.

The prisoner was lying on the cot, reading a book. Mattie watched as the woman read, only moving to turn the pages every few minutes.

Her mind began to wander, and she forced herself to pay attention. She studied the room, looking for the page they'd seen torn out. The book was a paperback and looked like urban fantasy, which meshed with the page they'd found in this cell.

They'd found it crumpled up at the foot of the cot, but it wasn't there yet in the scene.

Amy sped up the timing on the scene and the prisoner's movements got fast and jerky.

Suddenly, everything changed and Amy hurriedly paused the scene and changed it back to normal speed.

Mattie's gaze snapped to the woman's face as the mage threw her book across the room and sat up on the cot. Her eyes were completely black.

***

Tillie poked her head into another empty classroom, her white eyes seeing the present and the future, neither of which contained anything very interesting. She turned to call back out into the hallway. "Nothing here either. I think this is the last one, if we want to—"

Something unexpected entered her field of future vision. A book? Yes, a book floating in thin air. Not flying toward someone's head, like you'd expect if it were being used as a weapon. Just floating there. A new distraction, maybe?

She walked toward the corner it was about to float around, noting Trevor and Father Sean exchanging puzzled glances as both she and Giovani headed in the same direction.

"What's going on?" Trevor murmured as they passed.

"I don't know," said Giovani.

Tillie reached the corner first and peered around it. There was no one there, but she could see the book coming toward her in the present now.

"What the . . . ?" said Father Sean right behind her.

Tillie watched as Trevor reached forward and grabbed the book with one hand. It slipped straight through his grasp, not hurrying, just gliding by.

Frowning, Trevor seized the book with both hands. It began pulling him inexorably down the hall. Again, in no hurry, but apparently with great strength.

Gasping, Trevor let go and it continued on its way.

Tillie just stood there staring, completely flummoxed, as Father Sean started to limp after it.

"Come on, you guys!" he called over his shoulder. "We have to see where it's going!"

"It might be a trap!" Giovani protested.

"Or we might be letting them get away with something if we don't follow," Tillie pointed out. She hurried to catch up with the one-legged priest and the book.

Trevor followed, but when Tillie glanced back, Giovani still stood, uncertainly, in the middle of the corridor.

She paused. "Come on, Giovani, we need to stick together. Sister Margaret was adamant about that. And I don't think anything's going to stop Father Sean from getting to the bottom of this mystery!"

Giovani reluctantly jogged toward her.

Tillie grabbed his hand and together they ran down the hall toward the new corner Trevor and Father Sean had already turned.

Tillie extended her seer sight around the bend and stopped short at the sight she beheld.

Right in front of the door they were supposed to be guarding was a huge cluster of books, all floating in mid-air, as though waiting for someone. Or something.

***

Every cell was the same, albeit with a shorter and shorter space of time spent watching the prisoner reading. Mattie and her team watched as prisoner after prisoner read until they suddenly sat up and threw the book across the room, their eyes turning black.

Then they would stand, stiffly, like they were in a trance. They would walk mechanically over to where the book had landed, open it up to a random page, and tear it out.

Once the page was out, they'd drop it, close the book, and stand there, holding the tome to their chests for a few seconds, eyes still creepily inky.

And then they would disappear. Just vanish into thin air.

The book would remain in place for a moment, hovering right at the same level it had been clutched to the chest of the Auditor, and then it would float serenely toward the door. And the door would open and the book would float calmly out of the scene.

It happened in every cell, apparently simultaneously.

As the group went from cell to cell, watching this happen over and over, they got more and more frustrated. What the hell did it mean?

Sister Margaret was starting to slam the doors, her face grim and her breathing strained. Even Ida had stopped making snarky comments, and Amy seemed withdrawn and panicky.

Mattie didn't know what to think. She'd never seen anything like this, but then again, she was new to magery. She tended to gauge the severity of any given situation on the reactions of the more experienced mages around her.

And these reactions didn't bode well.

At least the spell Amy was under hadn't activated – the only black eyes they'd seen had been in the scenes of the courtiers.

Finally, they reached the first cell they'd gone to, which was actually the one that had been occupied for the least amount of time – just yesterday, Mattie had brought in the agent she'd laughingly dubbed Steve, and he had been put in this cell.

"This one didn't have a page torn out," said Amy, her voice weak and wavery. "Maybe this one will be different."

"Watch closely," said Sister Margaret. Her voice was tempered steel. "There must be something different here, and it might be the key to figuring this whole fucking thing out."

Sister Margaret plunked the scrying stone down on the toilet tank without further ado, settling herself into position on the seat and staring into it, barely waiting for Amy to take up her post behind her.

Mattie glanced at Ida as the old woman settled herself on the cot once again. She looked exhausted, her face drawn and worried. Mattie opened her mouth to ask if Ida was okay and if there was anything she could do for her, but Sister Margaret was already starting to scry.

She cast the projection spell instead.

The familiar scene opened up on the wall, the cell with the four of them in it. As Amy stitched, the scene changed and Steve replaced them.

He wasn't reading. He was angrily pacing the cell, his lips moving. Mattie adjusted the spell to include sound.

"—and that little bitch trying to tell me what to do. ME!" he was muttering. "Does she know who the fuck I am? Does she know what I've done? Read a book, she says. Fuck books." He glanced at the forest green book that lay on the cot.

Mattie squinted at the cover, but couldn't make out the title. It was a plain hardback with no jacket, so it could have been any genre.

"Haven't read a book since high school and didn't want to read 'em then. Read a boo—" Suddenly he stiffened and his eyes went black. His face scrunched up as though he was trying to fight it. As his body moved mechanically toward the cot, he tripped, apparently over nothing, and went crashing to the floor.

Steve's eyes opened back up, no longer black, and he looked around his cell wildly. "What the hell just happened?" he demanded of the air around him. His head snapped around as the door to his cell silently opened.

He jumped to his feet and stepped over to peer into the hallway. "What the — What?" He stared out the door for a moment and then shook his head. "Well, whatever is happening, I'm getting out of here."

Steve stepped out the door and the alarms began to sound. A moment later, he came back into the cell, grabbed the book off the cot, and then strode back out into the hallway.

Sister Margaret kept the scene going, presumably to see if he'd come back in. Mattie kept the projection steady too.

After a minute of nothing happening, Sister Margaret switched off the scrying and Mattie dropped her spell. The four of them remained in their positions, silently sunk in thought.

"The alarms went off when he left his cell," said Amy.

"That's what they're supposed to do," Sister Margaret pointed out.

"No, I mean, at the exact moment *he* left *his* cell." Amy looked around at all of them. "He left after the invisible people carried their books out because he wasn't an automaton. None of the books hesitated, right? They just floated out. But he stood at the door and watched for a few seconds before he decided he was leaving. As soon as he left, the alarms went off."

Understanding dawned in Mattie's mind. "You're saying the others didn't trigger them for some reason."

"It has to be related to the books," said Sister Margaret, grimly. "Come on. We're going to replay the scene in the hallway too."

Ida's straight back slumped every so slightly.

Mattie cast a spell, creating a cushion of magic beneath Ida's rear end. "Don't worry about your levitation spell," she said. "I've got you."

"Thank you, dear," said Ida.

Mattie floated Ida out in front of her as they exited the cell and then deposited her, still on her airy chair, beside the wall.

***

It had been about twenty minutes and the cluster of books was still just hovering patiently in front of the exit. Tillie, Trevor, Giovani, and Father Sean had tried just about everything to move them.

Tugging on them didn't budge them. When Trevor tried to stitch them away, he got magical whiplash, leaving him with a massive headache that had yet to fade.

Father Sean had tried a wind spell, but, while the pages did flutter, the books remained put.

Tillie had opened a couple of them, but nothing seemed out of the ordinary about the books themselves – just their behavior.

"It would help to know if they were being spelled in place or stitched there," said Father Sean. He plopped himself down on the stairs opposite the big, wooden double doors with a pained look on his face.

Trevor looked concerned. "Is your leg bothering you?"

"A little bit," he said. "I'm not used to this much walking around. I know you can't do much for an old injury like this, but I wouldn't say no to a little pain management if you think you've got the time."

"Of course," said Trevor. He held out his hands toward Father Sean, starting a complex healing gesture.

Tillie turned her attention back to the books as Giovani began walking around and between them, looking at the hovering tomes from all angles. "I wonder if—" she began. She stopped, her eyes widening, as Giovani suddenly stiffened, right in the middle of the cluster.

His eyes went black and he stood perfectly still.

"Oh, fuck," said Trevor.

"Huh," said Tillie, staring at Giovani, who was still standing frozen in place, his eyes flooded with darkness. "It would be nice if Giovani's spell would just do the same thing twice in a row. A pattern, so we could figure out how to stop it."

Then Giovani's head did move. It swiveled on his neck until his unseeing black eyes stared straight at Tillie. "Jesus, fuck!" she yelped. "What is he trying to do?"

"I don't know," said Father Sean. "But we need to help him. Maybe if we can take a look at his energy right now, while he's gone black-eyed."

Trevor stitched, but nothing happened. "The scrying stone isn't in the classroom anymore," he said with a frown.

"I've got mine at home," said Tillie. She stitched the stone from her ritual room and looked around for a spot to set it. There was a small table against the wall beside the stairwell with some pamphlets about the school's arts program and a chair beside it. She strode to the table and threw the pamphlets on the floor, setting the stone down and settling herself on the chair.

"Ready?" she said. Without waiting for a response, she dove in, flipping her eyes to seer mode and peering at Giovani's energy system, trusting that Father Sean would project it onto the wall, and hoping that Trevor would be able to stitch the spell away somehow.

***

There wasn't anywhere to put the scrying stone in the hallway, so Sister Margaret had Ida hold it up as she stared into its depths.

Mattie projected the scene onto the wall, and they watched the empty hall for a while until a woman showed up. Mattie frowned. The woman looked vaguely familiar. She was a new recruit, right?

Very new. Just brought in a day or two ago.

"Polly?" said Amy, slowing down the scene so the woman moved normally. "What is she doing here?"

"You know her?" asked Sister Margaret.

"Yeah, Polly's been part of our movement for ages. I didn't know she was here."

Then Mattie remembered. "Tillie found her yesterday. That's right. She and her partner —"

"Her husband, Bernie," said Amy.

Mattie's eyebrows shot up. "Auditor agents are allowed to get married? I thought they just had affairs and then turned their offspring over to the court."

Amy shook her head. "No, they're not allowed to. Polly and Bernie did it anyway. I was at their wedding, actually. It was very nice. But very secret. Agent Miller pulled a bunch of strings to get them assigned to each other as partners."

"Isn't that sweet?" said Sister Margaret. "But what the fuck is she doing?"

The woman was furtively approaching each door and dropping something small outside.

Mattie walked to the nearest cell and picked up something red and porous. "A piece of brick?"

"It must have a spell embedded in it," said Sister Margaret, grimly. "Are we so sure this Polly person is on our side?"

Amy raised her hands defensively and the picture on the wall flickered back to the present as her stitching stopped. "I swear, I know her well. She would never do this! It has to be some kind of a trick."

"Get the picture back up," Sister Margaret ordered. "I want to see if her eyes are black."

Amy lowered her hands back to Sister Margaret's shoulders, and the scene went back to Polly and her tiny bricks.

Her eyes were perfectly normal.

9.

Tillie stared at Giovani's energy body. It looked exactly the same as it had in the classroom, except for his eyes, which were, predictably, jet black.

She felt Father Sean grab the picture and project it on the wall. She watched as Trevor began stitching, focusing on sweeping the strange energy free of his eyes.

"Is it just me or is this taking longer than it did this morning?" she asked after a while. Her energy was feeling drained and she wasn't sure how much longer she could hold the image. "Is anything changing at all?"

"It's not you," said Trevor through gritted teeth. "I don't think the spell was fighting me before. It's definitely fighting me now. I do see a difference, though. The eyes are murky grey instead of pure black. And it's changing faster with each stitch I do. Look, the rest of his energy is connected to those eyes."

Tillie saw immediately what he meant. Even though Trevor was focusing solely on the eyes, other areas of Giovani's energy body were healing along with them.

"We need reinforcements," said Father Sean. "I'll let Sister Margaret know."

Out of the corner of her eye, Tillie saw Father Sean typing on his phone. At least the projection spell was relatively straightforward, so he could do both at the same time.

Staring into the scrying stone, she could see that the throat chakra, which had been one of the worst spots, was finally starting to slow a little from its mad spinning. It was still an angry red color and it still kept switching up its direction at random intervals, but it was a start.

Father Sean's phone chirped. "She's assigning another team to take over her sector and her team is coming to help." The phone chirped again. "Oh. She's asking about floating books. And someone named Polly. Does anyone know a Polly?"

Tillie didn't respond, as she was at the end of her reserves and needed all her focus to hold the image of Giovani's energy. The name sounded familiar, but she couldn't place it.

Not a moment too soon, she heard running footsteps pounding around the corner. Then hands landed on her shoulders and she felt Sister Margaret's energy course through her. The nun deftly took over the scrying as well.

Gratefully, Tillie relaxed, inhaling and exhaling deeply.

Amy slid to a halt next to Trevor. "What can I do?" she asked.

"Take the left eye," he said. "I'll focus on the right. Just the eyes – it seems to be helping everything."

Amy's fingers began to move and glow and Tillie could see a visible difference in how quickly Giovani was healing.

Tillie was a little surprised at how quickly it happened. Amy must be as powerful as Trevor, then. And Trevor was one of the strongest stitchers Tillie had ever seen.

Of course, Amy was a fully-trained stitcher and Trevor was still a beginner.

Ida, floating in an invisible chair, slid over beside Father Sean. Mattie sat between the two of them, a hand on each shoulder, probably sending mage energy into them both.

Tillie frowned slightly. She was used to thinking of Ida as an invincible force of nature, and this tired old woman looked like a completely different person.

As Mattie poured energy into the elderly speller, however, she began to look more like herself.

Tillie supposed she had just pushed herself too hard the past few days. She made a mental note to insist that Ida get some rest as soon as today was over.

They could manage without her for a while.

Giovani's chakras were now showing some real signs of progress and his meridians had brightened to an almost ordinary yellow. Tillie risked a glance over at Giovani's physical form. His face had followed her when she'd moved to the chair, and he still stared directly at her with his blank, black-filled eyes.

Tillie shivered. Was that significant in some way? And if so, did it have anything to do with the fact that she and Giovani had been getting closer?

Or was it related to the spell itself and whoever the hell had cast it?

She wasn't sure she wanted to know. Well, she definitely wanted to know if it was the former. She didn't want to know if it had to do with some malevolent mage who could do things no one had ever seen before and was suddenly showing an interest in her, of all people.

If that was the case, she could do without the knowledge. Oh, who was she kidding? Of course, she would want to know that. Forewarned is forearmed.

Still.

Those black eyes were super fucking creepy.

Tillie looked back at the projection of his energy body and saw that his eyes looked normal and his chakras and meridians looked almost healthy.

Trevor and Amy made a few more sweeps and then stepped back. His form glowed a healthy gold, the rivers flowing normally and the chakras spinning lazily.

Tillie held her breath.

Giovani's eyelids flickered and he collapsed in a heap.

Again.

***

Mattie leaped to her feet as Giovani crumped to the ground.

Again.

This poor bastard had been through the wringer lately. She sprinted over to his prone form, just ahead of her sister. She grabbed his wrist and felt his pulse jump.

Still alive, so that was a good start.

Together, Mattie and Tillie gently flipped him over onto his back, just as his eyes began blinking rapidly and he started to cough.

"Hey," said Tillie. "Take it easy. Do you remember anything about the last —" she glanced at her wrist " — hour?"

He shook his head, his cough subsiding. "All I know is that something was trying to get me to open the door, and there was no way in hell I was going to oblige it. I could feel that if I allowed myself to move my body at all, I would find myself opening the door. So I forced myself to focus on Tillie. As long as I focused on one thing other than the door, I was okay. And I could feel you working on me." He nodded toward the stitchers, who were crouched beside him as well. "I figured I could wait it out. Am I all better now?"

"I hope so," said Trevor. "No way to know for sure, but your chakras are back to normal."

Sister Margaret was pacing around them, staring at the floating books that still crowded around. She hissed. "But we still don't fucking know what the fuck these fucking books have to fucking do with anything." She paused and added, "Fuck!" for good measure.

Mattie couldn't help but grin. The situation was dire, but at least there were nuns in the world who swore like sailors.

Well, one at least.

Standing, Mattie joined Sister Margaret in studying the books, while Amy filled in the others on what they'd seen in the cells and the hallway.

"Wasn't Polly the woman who was missing?" said Trevor.

Tillie smacked herself in the forehead. "Yes! I knew the name was familiar. She's the one I brought in yesterday. The British woman with the financial hacker guy. And then he was saying his wife disappeared right before the alarms went off."

"But supposedly, she's not a stitcher," said Sister Margaret.

"Oh, so when you say she 'disappeared,'" said Mattie.

"Like she had stitched. We thought someone must have stitched her away," said Tillie. "But maybe she stitched herself because she's not who she says she is."

"I have a theory," said Ida.

Mattie was gratified to hear Ida's voice nearing its usual strident timbre. As she turned to face Ida, she saw that the woman's back was ruler-straight again as well and her eyes sharp.

Ida hopped down from the seat Mattie had made out of magic for her, and Mattie released the spell, glad to have one less suck on her energy.

As she spoke, Ida walked toward them. "I don't know this Polly from Adam, but either she's dead and someone else has taken her place, or you don't know her as well as you thought either and she's a traitor. Whichever it is, I think she dropped those bricks because they're bespelled, as you said. I think she dropped all of them and then set off the spell and skedaddled."

Ida reached the cluster of books and paused to study the one closest to her before continuing. "I think the spell itself was meant to put the essence of those courtiers into the books. That's why they ripped out a page. The theory there, I suppose, was that if a page was left behind, the alarms wouldn't go off because the occupant of the cell was still there, just a little bit." She tapped the cover of a hardcover book, setting it spinning.

"Hey, it's moving!" said Tillie. "We couldn't get them to budge before, except to open and close."

"Do you think the spell is fading?" asked Mattie. If the speller who cast it was getting tired, the spell could get weaker. It was probably a lot for one person to be holding.

"That's an interesting theory, Ida," said Sister Margaret. "But it's impossible. You can't put the essence of a person into an object. Can you?"

Ida shrugged. "Never discount magic, I always say. I've never seen anyone do it. But it's one of those urban legends, I suppose. I heard rumors as a girl of powerful mages who could do things like that. And the Auditors themselves are also an urban legend, remember."

"Okay, but why didn't it work on Steve?" asked Trevor.

"I never claimed I had all the answers," said Ida, tartly. "It's just a theory."

"Could it have something to do with Steve being an agent and not a courtier?" said Amy. "Maybe there's some kind of mental conditioning the court goes through that preps them for being used for a spell like this, similar to whatever made us agents more susceptible to the spell we were under."

"There were other agents in those cells," Trevor pointed out. "Anyone who showed up to report for duty at HQ in the past few days. Three of them, I think."

"Right," said Amy, deflated.

"It was a good thought, though," said Mattie.

"I think the most important question at hand," said Sister Margaret, "is how to stop these books from escaping and turning back into courtiers."

"Would they be able to leave?" Mattie frowned. "I thought the barrier spell prevented that."

Sister Margaret threw up her hands. "I have no fucking clue. I'm honestly out of my element here. Do books count as people? I don't know. I do know that even if they can't get through the spell, then unless I can figure out how to contain them in another way, I can't drop the spell and no one is getting in or out."

"They must have thought they could get out," said Giovani. "Or they wouldn't have been trying to get me to open the door for them."

"Was it the books?" said Tillie. "Or was it Polly?"

"This is ridiculous," said Amy. "Polly is a seer."

Ida put a hand on Amy's arm. "I'm sorry, dear, but I don't think that was Polly. I think Polly is dead, and I think—"

Suddenly Ida stopped talking and her hand clawed at her throat.

"Ida!" shouted Mattie, rushing to her side. Once she was there, though, there was nothing she could do. "What's going on?"

"Spell," Ida gasped, her voice raspy and almost inaudible. "Choking...."

Mattie spun around, searching for the speller, the others in the group doing the same, fanning out to find the hidden mage. They had to be nearby – you couldn't cast a spell on someone you couldn't see.

Then again, no one thought you could put the essence of a person into a book either.

"Up there!" Mattie saw a shadowy figure pressed against the wall at the top of the stairs, a telltale glow shining where the speller's hands were.

She sprinted up the stairs, throwing magical fireballs as she ran. The flames hit a shield that spread across the stairwell and dissipated.

Mattie aimed lightning at the wall, chipping away at the cinder block to create a chink outside of the shield. Finally, a large enough piece flew away, and Mattie tossed a tiny fireball, sending it directly at the speller.

A curse came from the figure and the shield wavered, just long enough for Sister Margaret, who was right behind Mattie to throw a well-aimed, perfectly-timed dagger right through the gap and into the throat of the mage.

The shield fell and Mattie took the rest of the stairs in two huge bounds, skidding to a halt beside the fallen woman. "Agent Shezza!" she exclaimed. "What the hell?"

She took the mage's wrist in her own and felt a very faint pulse.

"Keep her alive, if you can," said Sister Margaret. "I have questions."

Mattie put a stasis spell over Agent Shezza, freezing her before she lost any more blood. "I thought she was dead. And on our side. Was she impersonating Polly?"

"She must have been," said Sister Margaret. She turned around and called down the stairs. "I need a stitcher up here."

Amy jogged up toward them. "Shezza?" she said when she reached the top. Her voice was filled with the same disbelief Mattie felt. "But she died in the fire last week. And she's an idiot."

"Apparently not," said Mattie. "Can you get her stabilized so we can question her?"

"Yeah, sure." Amy knelt beside the fallen mage. "You have a spell on her?"

"Should I release it?" asked Mattie.

"On three," said Amy. She readied her hands for a stitch. "One. Two. Three."

As Mattie released her stasis spell, Amy moved her fingers. Sister Margaret's knife flew out of the wound and it quickly closed.

"Now put the spell back," said Sister Margaret, catching her dagger and wiping it clean on a piece of fabric. "Until we're ready for her. How is Ida doing?"

"She's not dead," said Amy. "Trevor's working on repairing any damage to her throat."

Mattie's hands glowed as she levitated Agent Shezza. She stood and began walking back down the stairs, hauling the mage behind her.

Sister Margaret and Amy followed.

When she reached the atrium, she found an argument going on.

"I remember when you were just a baby, toddling on your father's knee, and I'll be damned if I'm going to let you tell me what I can and cannot do, little boy," Ida was saying to Giovani. The effect was slightly ruined by the fact that she could barely get the words out through her ravaged throat. "I am perfectly capable of—"

"No one is saying you're not capable, Ida," said Tillie in a soothing voice.

Ida pivoted to face her. "You're going to interrupt me, you little upstart? You little tart? You started this whole thing, and I am going to—"

"Yes, I am interrupting you!" said Tillie, her voice rising in volume. "You know damn well that you wouldn't let anyone else in your current state do what you're saying you can do! We're all aware of who you are and what you've done and what you can do. But you're exhausted and injured and you should be resting."

Ida drew herself up to her full height and opened her mouth to speak. Then she closed it again, bowing her head. "You're right," she said. "When you're right, you're right. I wouldn't let anyone else push themselves the way I've been pushing myself. I'm getting too old for this. Maybe it's time I retired from the warrior life."

"No one's saying you have to retire, Auntie," said Giovani affectionately. "Just get some rest." He turned to Sister Margaret. "Is there a spare bed somewhere around here?"

"Of course," she replied. She turned to Ida. "You know where the infirmary is, don't you?"

"Sure," said Ida. "I've never had to be in there myself, but I've visited."

"We know," said Mattie. "You're invincible."

"Apparently not," said Ida.

"Someone should go with you," said Father Sean.

"I'll go," Mattie volunteered. "If someone else can take over this stasis spell."

"Actually…." Sister Margaret looked up at the ceiling.

Mattie followed her gaze and saw a black square marked across two tiles.

"Put her under that," Sister Margaret directed her.

Mattie pushed Agent Shezza into the square and as soon as the rogue agent entered the spot, four pulsing, translucent walls came crashing down around them.

"Don't worry," said Sister Margaret. "It'll only hold her – you've got the pendant."

Mattie reached up to touch the symbol hanging around her neck, the flaming sword of the nuns' order. She stepped out of the cage spell and released the stasis spell holding Agent Shezza.

Agent Shezza crumpled to the ground once again.

Then Mattie took Ida's arm and began walking her toward the convent.

***

"What do you think?" said Sister Margaret. "Is she well enough to interrogate?"

Amy shrank slightly under the warrior nun's regard. "I guess that depends on what you mean by interrogate," she said. Her voice sounded very nervous. "And whether you expect her to survive the process."

Sister Margaret's lips twitched. "Relax. This isn't the Spanish Inquisition. I'm not going to torture anyone. I just want to ask her a few questions."

"I tried torturing her once, actually," said Tillie. "It didn't work."

"You what?" stammered Amy.

"Well, we were mostly just trying to make her think we were going to torture her," said Trevor. He shook his head at Tillie. "Let's not give this poor woman a heart attack."

Tillie grinned back at him.

"Thank you," Amy murmured. "I'm afraid I'm not cut out for this kind of excitement. As long as you're not going to torture her, I think as soon as she regains consciousness, she should be good for some light questioning."

"In the meantime," said Giovani. "We have a few things we need to figure out." He began to tick them off on his fingers. "First of all, how to get these books contained so that we can extract the essence of those courtiers from them—"

"I'm not convinced that's what's happened," said Sister Margaret. "As far as I know, it's impossible. I've never heard these rumors Ida was talking about."

"I have," said Father Sean. "Not recently. Everyone these days is much more sensible than that. But when I was a kid, which would have been about twenty years after Ida was a kid, I heard stories about that kind of thing. And what's more, I heard it in direct conjunction with stories about secret societies. My uncle said the Knights Templar could do it, along with all kinds of other crazy things, like using more than one discipline of magery—" he looked pointedly at Giovani as he said that, "and turn people into animals, which I know for a fact that witches can do."

"We're not talking about witches," said Sister Margaret. "You can't combine witchcraft and magery. Everyone knows—" She stopped herself and grimaced. "Okay, so we can't rely on what everyone knows. That's fair. But the whole 'these books contain peoples' essenses' thing is still only a theory and I think it's important that we don't get distracted assuming it's the only possible explanation!"

Tillie glanced over at Agent Shezza and saw that the woman's eyes were open just a slit and she was glaring around at all of them while trying to pretend she was still asleep. "She's awake!"

"Fantastic!" said Sister Margaret. "Let's get to questioning."

Agent Shezza sat up and immediately tried to throw a fireball at Sister Margaret, ducking as it reflected back to her. "Fair enough," said the agent.

Her voice was different than it had sounded the last time Tillie had spoken with her. It was deeper and somehow carried more inflection. A more intelligent voice.

Sister Margaret strode to the edge of the slight blur that delineated the mirrored cage spell. "You're supposed to be dead," she said. "What gives?"

Agent Shezza sighed. "I guess my disguise didn't survive the alarms, then? That's a shame. I liked being Polly. Polly was such a simple person."

"What did you do with her?" Amy demanded.

"Killed her," said Agent Shezza smugly, as she leaned back on her elbows. "Slit her precious little throat about, let's see, four days ago now."

Trevor put a comforting arm around Amy as she turned away, holding in a sob.

Agent Shezza laughed. "Oh, Amy. Such a sweet little idiot. Not as dumb as my Agent Shezza character, of course. But really, quite silly."

"So, Agent Shezza was a traitor after all," murmured Tillie.

"Of course not," said Shezza. "Don't be ridiculous. Agent Shezza was an idiot, but you've never met her. She slipped up almost immediately, before that actual traitor Agent Miller ever spoke to her in person, allowing me to take her place in your paltry little rebellion."

"Not that paltry," said Giovani. "We took down the court, didn't we?"

"Did you?" Shezza raised an eyebrow and pointedly turned her head to regard the floating books.

"We killed the Pontiff," said Amy.

"Did you?" said Shezza again.

"I'll ask the fucking questions," Sister Margaret snarled.

"Suit yourself." Agent Shezza flipped over onto her stomach and began doing push-ups.

Tillie watched, impressed in spite of herself. She was strong, but she couldn't do push-ups this fast. And that was a hell of a cool move – doing push-ups while trapped in a mirror spell and being questioned.

Sister Margaret just rolled her eyes. "Let's start with your actual name."

"That is none of your business." Shezza didn't even pause in her workout. And her voice showed no sign of strain.

"It is if you want us to go easy on you," said Sister Margaret, crouching to Shezza's level. "You've probably concluded that we're not going to torture you, and that's correct. But that's just us. I can hand you over to any number of people who don't share my compassion. The Catholic Church has gotten a lot less brutal in the past couple hundred years. But that's only compared to how we used to be."

Now Shezza did pause, but only to lift one hand, continuing her push-ups one-handed with her left arm stretched upward and her body turned toward Sister Margaret. She refrained from answering.

"Have you ever heard of Cardinal Neubacher?" asked Sister Margaret, casually.

Tillie hadn't, but she watched Shezza's face carefully, and there was a split second there where it was clear that she *had* heard of him and that what she'd heard wasn't good.

Then her face smoothed out and she lowered her arm, lifting the other and turning away to continue her push-ups on the other side before responding. "There is no Cardinal Neubacher. Do you think I'm a child? Or a gullible fool?"

"I promise you, he is very real," said Sister Margaret, softly.

Tillie shivered at her tone. Something made her glance over at Father Sean, and the stricken look on his face told her everything she needed to know about this Cardinal. "I don't think it needs to come to that," she said.

If Father Sean was that terrified of this person, she certainly wasn't going to hand anyone over to him, even Shezza. "Why don't you just tell us what you're doing here?" she said.

Shezza snorted. "If you can't even figure that out, we've grossly underestimated you. And to be frank, we didn't have that high an opinion to start."

"Okay, so you're here to spring the remnants of the court free," said Sister Margaret. "That's clear. Who sent you?"

"The Pontiff, of course," said Shezza. She finished her pushups and jumped to her feet, stretching luxuriously upward. Her fingers brushed the mirror shield and Tillie saw Amy wince slightly as it zapped her with a spark of lightning.

Shezza didn't even flinch, but she did acknowledge Amy's discomfort with a small twitch of her lips.

Tillie stepped up beside Amy, silently lending her support. If there was one thing she couldn't stand, it was a bully.

She met Shezza's eyes, staring her down, and the prisoner's smile widened.

"The Pontiff is dead," said Giovani, flatly. "Ida Garavelli cut off his head last Friday."

"Did she?" Shezza began to move through a series of Tai Chi poses.

Tillie stepped forward again. Sister Margaret shouldn't be doing this all on her own. Shezza was clearly clever enough to need a two-pronged attack, at the very least.

The best way to conduct an interrogation without resorting to actual torture was to play on the person's weaknesses. What were Shezza's weaknesses?

Hubris, maybe? She seemed pretty confident.

So. Keep things vague and conversational, and maybe she'd let something slip. She was too smart to answer a direct question, but leading statements might work.

"Let's say he isn't dead," said Tillie. "Let's say you know something we don't—"

"I know lots of things that you don't," said Shezza.

"And you're saying the Pontiff is alive?" said Trevor.

"Did I say that?" asked Shezza.

Tillie tried to steer the conversation back to vague. "If we were to speculate that perhaps the Pontiff managed to survive being beheaded, I wonder where the Pontiff would be right now."

"No one can survive a beheading, you silly goose," said Shezza.

Sister Margaret seemed to catch on to Tillie's strategy. "So, maybe that wasn't the Pontiff who Ida beheaded at all."

"It sure looked like the Pontiff," said Trevor.

Tillie caught his eye and smiled. Maybe he was starting to get it too. She just hoped Amy didn't try to jump in. It's not that Amy wasn't smart, but she was really more of an accountant than an interrogator.

"Well, of course, it looked like him," Shezza laughed. "What else would you have expected?"

It was working! Tillie stifled the uncharacteristic urge to let out a triumphant cackle. Keep it going…. Shezza's weakness was clearly her hubris.

"I suppose you're right," said Tillie. "I am a silly goose." She slumped slightly as though ashamed of herself.

"So, if, as you theorize, they just had someone dressed up like the Pontiff," said Giovani slowly, as though piecing it all together, "then that would mean that the Pontiff is still out there, and could be putting this darn spell on all of us who used to be loyal agents and have lost our way."

Tillie thought this was laying it on a little bit thick, but Shezza's grin just grew, so maybe it was right.

"Or triggering a spell that was put on you before you lost your way," said Sister Margaret in a chiding voice. "After all, he does know best, doesn't he? He could have thought ahead."

"Yes!" said Shezza. Her eyes had a fanatical light to them as she abandoned her exercises and began jumping up and down. "We thought of everything! You idiots have no idea who you're dealing with! The organization has been around for hundreds of years! We have knowledge and forethought you can't even imagine!"

"How could we ever hope to beat an organization like that?" Tillie moaned.

"You can't," said Shezza. She paced her spelled cage like a tiger. A gleeful tiger, about to burst with smugness. "You can never win. We will take back our children and we will start our court anew as we've done every other time anyone has tried to fight us. We have reinforcements descending upon you from all over the world. You think you've won? You think this one paltry attack can beat us down? You can't even imagine the hellfire that is about to rain down on you in just one week!"

One week? Tillie's breath caught. What was going to happen in a week? She forced herself not to say anything. Just wait it out. Shezza had to have more to say.

Shezza put her hands out, leaning against the sizzling wall of her pen as though they were just bars of a prison cell. As though her palms weren't blistering and bubbling from the heat of the spell.

She stared straight at Tillie with the intensity of a shark. Or a serial killer. "You are all going to die." She stepped closer to the wall, the skin of her hands bright red.

Blisters were forming, yellow bubbles as her skin seemed to be boiling, parts of her palms even starting to blacken.

Tillie found herself mesmerized by the woman's hands. How was she doing this? Why was she doing this? She was going to lose her hands. Wasn't she a stitcher? She wouldn't be able to stitch without hands.

The hands were moving. Agent Shezza spread her arms and leaned her entire body up against the wall of the spell. Her clothing began to smoke. Tillie stood, frozen, staring at her. What the hell was she doing?

"Somebody put up another shield!" yelled Sister Margaret.

Giovani responded immediately, his hands glowing, a new cage appearing inside of the automatic one, this one without the mirror spell aspect of it.

The new cage was much smaller, forcing Agent Shezza to stand up straight, her hands braced against it with her arms forced into a cactus-like position. It made her look like she had surrendered.

This impression was belied by the way Agent Shezza laughed wildly as she leaned back slightly. "I guess one of you has some sense, not to let the prisoner die before you have a chance to hand her over to the real interrogator." Her eyes darted over to study Sister Margaret. "Well? When do we go to see Cardinal Neubacher, if there is such a person?"

"We don't have time," said Father Sean, curtly. "Not if they're sending an army within a week. Cardinal Neubacher is very good, but he does like to take his time."

"We can still send her," said Sister Margaret. There was a coldness to her voice that Tillie hadn't never heard from her before. "You never know how quickly someone can break. And every little piece of information is worthwhile." Sister Margaret put her face very close to Shezza's. "You were willing to kill yourself rather than reveal more information. That was a mistake. It tells us that you have secrets worth more than your life. The good Cardinal will happily walk that line."

Shezza grinned at her. "But in the meantime, how will you prepare for our army? You can't even stop a bunch of books from escaping your little school."

Sister Margaret gestured toward the group of floating books. "We seem to be managing. They haven't escaped yet."

"Maybe we should just set them on fire," suggested Giovani. He walked toward the books, flicking one of the covers. "Or just rip out all of the pages and scatter them to the wind. How would you be able to recover them?" He grinned hugely. "No pun intended."

Tillie watched her friends carefully. She couldn't tell anymore if they were bluffing or not. Her eyes met Amy's.

Maybe she had more in common with the timid stitcher than she thought. Killing in battle was one thing, but what Giovani was discussing was outright murder, and Tillie had never crossed that line.

But she'd seen him do it – he had killed Agent Shezza's former partner in cold blood, while he was tied to a chair.

And then there was Sister Margaret, who was going to turn Shezza over to someone who sounded like a monster. Which amounted to murder, but more slowly, which was worse.

Trevor stepped closer to Tillie, taking her hand. Whatever happened, she and Trevor had always been there for each other.

She squeezed his hand, taking comfort in his presence and hoping he gained some from her as well.

Tillie glanced back toward Agent Shezza and found the captive spy watching her. Swallowing hard, Tillie glanced away again, looking at Father Sean instead.

Father Sean's lips were tightened in a flat line, as though he was holding back protests. As though he had hoped it wouldn't come to this, but wasn't going to stop it.

"Wait," said Agent Shezza, quietly. "There are pieces of our buildings outside the doors of all of the cells the court escaped from. Bring me them and I'll separate the courtiers from their books. You don't have to destroy them."

Sister Margaret smiled gently. "Good choice. Amy? Will you stitch the bricks here, please?"

Amy's hands moved quickly.

Tillie dropped Trevor's hand and started taking the small chunks of brick from Amy as she stitched them in, one at a time.

Trevor stitched in a bowl and Tillie filled it up with chunks of brick.

Each piece was about the size of an apricot.

Once they were all collected, she stepped toward Agent Shezza with the bowl. This was almost certainly a trap and she didn't trust the woman as far as she could stitch her, but right now there were two layers of shield between them.

For good measure, Tillie set a personal shield between the hand that held the bowl and the rest of herself, unsure whether Sister Margaret and Giovani would have to drop their cages.

Shezza grinned at her. "Come on, girl. I'm not going to bite."

"Biting isn't really what I'm worried about," Tillie said, dryly.

"I need to touch the bricks," said Shezza.

Of course she did. This was feeling more and more like a certain trap by the moment.

"Shields up, everybody," murmured Father Sean. "Remember, we outnumber her."

Tillie put up a shield around Trevor too and saw Father Sean do the same for Amy.

Sister Margaret probably didn't need one, but Tillie put one up around her anyway.

"Can I get a sound shield between us and her?" said Sister Margaret.

The glow around Giovani's hands pulsed as he put it up.

Okay," said Sister Margaret. She turned to Amy. "Take off your necklace, please. When I give the word, you'll stitch it into Shezza's hand. That's the only way to lower the mirror cage, but I want to do it suddenly and hope it catches her off-guard. Giovani, you'll drop your cage at the same time. Everyone, be ready for whatever bullshit she's going to pull. Sound shield down."

Giovani's glow pulsed again as he dropped one of his spells.

"Amy, now," said Sister Margaret.

Amy's hands moved in a stitch and her necklace appeared above Shezza, who caught it reflexively.

Giovani's hands stopped glowing right after, and Shezza stumbled backward as the spell-wall she was leaning against fell.

"We're watching you," Giovani warned. "One false move and you're dead."

"Along with my secrets," she said, regaining her balance and stepping forward.

"So be it." He nodded soberly. "My friends' lives are worth more than yours."

Shezza's lips curved upward in a sly smile. "Noted."

Tillie levitated the bowl of bricks toward her.

"Just undo the spell," said Sister Margaret, her swords ready and her eyes seer-white. "Now."

***

Mattie and Ida walked in silence for a few minutes, Ida navigating them through the maze-like old building toward their eventual goal of the convent infirmary.

As they left the school section and entered the convent, the halls were lined with cozy reading nooks and studies full of antique furniture, interspersed among closed doors labeled with nun's names, which Mattie took to be bedrooms.

"I never thought I'd get this old, I suppose, dear," said Ida suddenly. Her voice was clearer now, even with just a small amount of resting it. "And I'm a bit flummoxed to find it so. I think everyone expected me to die young. Always getting into scrapes, throwing myself into fights, defending anyone who I thought needed defending. Or avenging."

Mattie smiled. "You got good at surviving."

"I suppose I did," said Ida with an answering smile. "But it won't be long now. I'm no seer, but I can feel it. I've had my time and it's coming to an end."

"Well, I've been learning to become a seer," said Mattie. "And I think you've got plenty of fight left in you."

Ida shook her head. "You're not a natural seer. You can't instinctively know what's coming. You'll never live in the future the way a natural would, even if you become as good a seer as your sister. But maybe you'll get close. You're more in balance now that you're practicing multiple disciplines. I can tell. It's funny, isn't it? The Auditors say that you're throwing the Universe off-balance by practicing outside your discipline, but really you become more stable, I suppose."

"That is funny," said Mattie. "Not that it makes me laugh. I almost wish I could go back to before I ever found out that mages are real. Before everything got fucked up."

"Do you?" Ida paused, turning toward Mattie to study her face. "I don't think you do. You've grown, dear, even in such a short time. Don't discount that."

Mattie's phone began to vibrate in her pocket and she pulled it out. It was her ex-husband again, not anyone in the building with them, so she put it back, turning back to her conversation with Ida.

As she turned, it was like the world went into slow motion. She heard a scream of rage from behind them and changed direction, spinning to face that way.

Mattie tried to throw her body in between Ida's and the young man hurtling toward her, his foot kicking toward Ida's head.

As the man danced back from Ida, Mattie punched him in the stomach.

She saw Ida falling to the ground and reached toward her to catch her, but had to twist again to avoid the man as he reacted to her punch, trying to headbutt her.

Reaching for an antique-looking dagger that hung on the wall, Mattie stitched it into her fingers, slitting the man's throat before he could hit her again.

He collapsed beside Ida, blood flowing into a puddle beside the old speller.

Mattie knelt beside her friend, feeling her neck and then her wrist, desperately seeking a pulse.

10.

The next few minutes happened too fast for Tillie to really follow, even as she was expecting something to go wrong.

One moment, she was holding out a bowl filled with small pieces of brick, cautiously inching it closer to Agent Shezza.

The next second, the bricks were flying through the air.

As they hit the walls, they shattered. Most of the ones that hit the floor didn't – they just skidded around, following their momentum.

Tillie took an involuntary step backward and found herself falling. She crashed to the ground, somehow, miraculously, instinctively covering her head with the wooden bowl that had contained the brick pieces.

Her neck recoiled as the bowl over her head hit the hard tiles and her brain felt rattled about, but she recovered, sitting up and watching the chaos around her, looking for an opening to help someone.

There – Agent Shezza was flying through the air toward Sister Margaret, who had her feet braced on the floor, her swords ready, her face lit in a bloodthirsty grin.

And over there – Trevor and Amy were still on their feet, but huddled together, heads sheltered in their arms as rubble careened around the atrium at deadly speeds. Tillie strengthened her shields, including the one over Trevor, expanding it to include another one around Amy.

Giovani had levitated himself to avoid the bricks scattered about the hall, and he strode over the air, surrounded by a shield of his own, headed toward Sister Margaret to help fight the Auditor agent, who had just reached the seer and was holding her own against her twin swords, both women's eyes white in seer mode.

Tillie's jaw clenched at the sight – she'd now seen Shezza stitch, spell, and see, all in the name of a secret society that claimed to do so was to be an Abomination.

Father Sean stood back, leaning against the wall, flinging lightning bolts at Agent Shezza, who avoided them as deftly as she avoided Sister Margaret's blades.

Tillie pulled herself to her feet, switching her own eyes into seer mode, preparing to join in the fray.

***

Mattie sobbed as Sister Helen covered Ida in a crisp white sheet.

"Shhhhh, it's okay," said another nun, wrapping Mattie in a hug. Mattie could feel the nun's hot tears falling on her shoulder, even as her own tears flowed freely down her face. "It was a warrior's death, fitting for one such as Ida Garaveldi."

"It was so meaningless," Mattie murmured.

"Nothing is meaningless," the nun said. "And you have avenged her already. She would have wanted that."

Mattie nodded, stepping back from the embrace and studying the corpse of the man she had killed.

At least another Auditor was dead.

It was anything but a fair trade.

Mattie's tears dried up as she glared at the man's still form, at the blood that pooled around his head and neck, wishing fiercely that she'd killed him more slowly.

If she'd known that Ida was already dead, she would have.

Mattie's angry heart gained fire with every beat. "Ida has not yet been avenged," she said, slowly. "All of these bastards will pay for her death. Every single last one of them."

And she could do that best by returning to the door where the court floated in front of a door they couldn't breach, in a form that was very, very flammable.

Mattie summoned a fireball. She held the ball of fire in her hand as her lips curved in a tiny, savage smile and she pivoted on her heel, heading back toward the action.

***

Tillie kicked Shezza in the back of the neck, impressed again, despite herself, by the woman's fighting prowess. How was she holding her own against Tillie, Sister Margaret, and Giovani?

Suddenly, there was Mattie, back at last, her face cold and emotionless as she strode toward the floating books, her own eyes seer white as well as she ducked and danced around the flying bricks, a fireball held in her hand.

Even Agent Shezza paused, arrested by the look on Mattie's usually-genial face.

Tillie watched as her sister calmly pulled her hand back and flung the fireball at the books. It hit one tome and it went up in flames immediately. A very human wail filled the air.

Mattie's hate-filled smile grew as she threw another fireball.

"Mattie!" shouted Trevor. "There are people trapped in those books!"

"They killed her," said Mattie calmly. She began throwing fireballs with both hands, each one hitting a book with unfailing accuracy. "They killed Ida."

"What?" Tillie stared at her sister, hoping she'd heard wrong.

Mattie kept throwing until every book was aflame and the air was filled with screams. Then she sat down on the floor with a thud, her body wracked with sobs.

Tillie was abruptly certain of one thing: she was tired of all of this. She formed a spell in her mind, for once doing it without even needed to murmur the words, and scooped up the few pieces of brick that were still flying around, forming them into a ball.

She threw the ball at Agent Shezza's head, and they hit hard, pummeling her face into a bloody pulp before falling dully to the floor.

Agent Shezza also fell to the floor and Sister Margaret pulled some zip ties out of her pocket, beckoning to Amy and Giovani to come and help her.

Tillie made her careful way over to Mattie, sitting down beside her and snuggling up against her back, slipping her arms around her twin's waist and leaning against her shoulder.

Mattie's hands covered hers as the two of them cried together for a woman they'd loved and looked up to. A woman who had been strong and kind and silly and a goddamn force of nature.

Mattie had only known Ida for a few weeks, but Tillie knew she'd truly loved the old woman. Tillie had known her for years, but she'd only really gotten to know her well these past few weeks.

None of that mattered. Ida should have lasted forever.

She was Ida fucking Garaveldi.

A hand landed on Tillie's shoulder and she looked up at Sister Margaret's tear-streaked face. "I know you're grieving," Sister Margaret said, gruffly. "I am too. But Ida would want us to finish this."

Tillie nodded and stood up, reaching out a hand to help Mattie up too. "What is there to finish?" she asked. She nodded toward the door, where a pile of ash was all that remained of the books. The air around them rang with the silence left by the absence of the courtiers' screams. "They're dead."

She looked at Agent Shezza. She was unconscious, her face was barely recognizable, and her hands were almost invisible, wrapped up in zip ties as they were. "She's incapacitated."

Sister Margaret nodded. "But they aren't all dead. There's more out there. Including the Pontiff, if she's to be believed."

"What?" said Mattie, her voice shocked.

"It may have been a decoy," said Tillie.

Mattie let out a string of vicious and creative profanity.

Even Sister Margaret's eyebrows shot up. "That about covers it," she said.

"So, what's next?" asked Father Sean, limping over to join them. "Regroup and plan for this supposed army coming next week?"

"Yeah, I guess so," said Sister Margaret. She pulled her cell phone out of its pouch on her leather bandolier, clicking on an app and holding the phone up to her face like she was on speakerphone. As she began to speak, her words were projected over the school's intercom system, echoing throughout the halls. "I need a supermax cell ready for a highly dangerous prisoner. All the rest of today's enemies are dead and accounted for. Everyone, please convene in the gym for briefing, as soon as possible."

"What about the guy in the last cell?" asked Amy. "The one who didn't tear out his page?"

"Dead," said Mattie, closing her eyes.

Trevor put an arm around her, concern written across his face.

"Well, that's everyone, then," said Giovani. "All of the captives dead, plus one warrior who was worth every single one of them."

Tillie pondered that – how could lives be weighed against lives and some found to be worth a different price? Who decided? Then again, when it came to Ida, he was probably right.

Ida was worth everyone.

Acknowledgements

I find myself struggling with this section more and more with book I put out – not because no one contributes, but because my community grows and I simply cannot thank everyone.

Perhaps it's best to thank people in groups. Of course, I must acknowledge my husband, Zeb. Actually, that's lovely to do because this is the first book published with Zeb as my husband, instead of "partner." Thank you, Zeb, for all of your support!

And then there's Zeb's family, with whom we share a home. Thank you for your support and your patience and for keeping the volume down when you can.

My family needs a mention as well. My parents who buy my books, even when they're not their cup of tea. My cousins who listen to me ramble on about plot points and characters at family gatherings. Thank you!

And my writer's group. Always there to bounce ideas and give honest critique.

And my beta readers, of course! Thank you for reading and for being brutally honest when it just wasn't working.

You all rock.

About the Author

Anna McCluskey is an independent fantasy author known for her witty dialogue, whimsical storylines, and immersive style. Anna lives in rural Oregon with her husband and way too many pets and plants.

For information on upcoming projects, check out her website, www.theannafiles.com.

www.ingramcontent.com/pod-product-compliance
Lightning Source LLC
Chambersburg PA
CBHW021143190726
48288CB00008B/2804